Larry Carr, diamond expert, finds himself in need of psychiatric treatment. His doctor tells him to have a change of scene; to get away from his opulent surroundings, to go to Luceville, an industrial town of poverty, to engage himself in welfare work and so think of others rather than himself.

This seems to be sound advice, but Carr was not to know that by going to Luceville he was to become involved in a world of crime and with Rhea Morgan – a vicious, sensual thief, just out of prison ...

HAVE A CHANGE OF SCENE

Also by James Hadley Chase

AN ACE UP MY SLEEVE
LADY, HERE'S YOUR WREATH
THE JOKER IN THE PACK
WELL NOW MY PRETTY
THE WAY THE COOKIE CRUMBLES
NO ORCHIDS FOR MISS BLANDISH
DO ME A FAVOUR—DROP DEAD
COME EASY, GO EASY
BELIEVED VIOLENT
CONSIDER YOURSELF DEAD
MALLORY
HAVE THIS ONE ON ME

and published by Corgi Books

James Hadley Chase

Have a Change of Scene

CORGI BOOKS

HAVE A CHANGE OF SCENE
A CORGI BOOK 0 552 09648 2

Originally published in Great Britain by
Robert Hale & Co.

PRINTING HISTORY
Robert Hale edition published 1973
Corgi edition published 1974
Corgi edition reprinted 1977
Corgi edition reissued 1979
Corgi edition reissued 1986

This book is set in Plantin 10/10½ pt.

Corgi Books are published by Transworld Publishers Ltd.,
61-63 Uxbridge Road, Ealing, London W5 5SA,
in Australia by Transworld Publishers (Aust.) Pty. Ltd.,
26 Harley Crescent, Condell Park, NSW 2200, and in New
Zealand by Transworld Publishers (N.Z.) Ltd., Cnr. Moselle
and Waipareira Avenues, Henderson, Auckland.

Made and printed in Great Britain by
Hunt Barnard Printing Ltd., Aylesbury, Bucks.

HAVE A CHANGE OF SCENE

ONE

It didn't begin to show until a month after the crash. You could call it delayed shock although Dr. Melish didn't call it that, but he is stuck with his technical jargon which is so much blah to you and me: a delayed shock is what he meant.

A month before the crash I was floating in the rarefied air of success. Take my job for instance. I had slaved for it and I finally got it: first salesman with the most exclusive jewellers in Paradise City: Luce & Fremlin. They are in the same bracket as Cartiers and Van Cleff & Arpels. In this city every store, shop, gallery and jewellers strive to be the best because this city is a millionaire's playground, where the snobs, the bulging-with-money boys, the film stars and the show-offs make it a backdrop for their display of wealth.

Luce & Fremlin are the best in their line and being their diamond expert gave me a salary of $60,000 a year which even in this city with its cost of living the highest on the Florida coast, was good money.

I owned a Mercedes convertible, a two-bedroom apartment overlooking the sea, a healthy bank balance and some $80,000 worth of Stocks and Bonds.

I had a wardrobe of good clothes. I was tall, said to be handsome and the best golfer and squash-racket player at the Country Club. Now maybe you will see what I mean when I say I was a man on a cloud of success ... but wait: to cap all this I had Judy.

I mention Judy last because she was (note the past tense) my most important possession.

Judy was brunette, pretty, intelligent and kind. We met at

7

the Country Club and I found she played a good game of golf. If I gave her six strokes, she would beat me and as I play down to −1 that meant she played a good game of golf. She had come from New York to Paradise City to research for material for old Judge Sawyer's autobiography. She quickly settled down in Paradise City, became popular and within a few weeks was an integral part of the young community at the club. It took me four weeks and about thirty rounds of golf to discover that Judy was my girl. She told me later it took her considerably less time to discover I was her man. We got engaged.

When my boss, Sydney Fremlin, who was one of those big hearted, slightly overwhelming homosexuals who—if he likes you—can't do enough for you, heard about the engagement, he insisted on throwing a party, Sydney loved parties. He said he would take care of the financial end and the party must be at the club and everyone—but everyone—invited. I didn't really want it, but it seemed to tickle Judy, so I went along.

Sydney knew I was about the best diamond man in the business, that without me the high standard of his shop would fall—rather like the standard of a *** Michelin French restaurant falls when the chef walks out—that all his clients liked me, consulted me and took my advice, so that made me very popular with Sydney, and when one is popular with Sydney he can't do enough.

That was a month ago. I look back on the evening of the party like a man, driven crazy with toothache, grinds down on the aching tooth.

Judy came to my apartment around 1900. The party wasn't due to begin until 2100, but we had arranged to meet early because we wanted to discuss what kind of house we were going to live in when we married. We had three choices: a ranch-type house with a big garden, a penthouse and a wooden chalet out of the city. I dug for the penthouse, but Judy leaned towards the ranch house because of the garden. We spent an hour or so discussing pros and cons, but finally, Judy convinced me a garden was essential.

'When the kids come, Larry ... we'll need a garden.'

8

There and then I had called Ernie Trowlie, the real-estate man we were dealing with and told him I'd be in tomorrow to pay the deposit on the ranch house.

We left my apartment feeling on top of the world and headed for the Country Club. A mile out of the city, and as we drove along the freeway my world came unstuck at the seams. A car shot out of a side turning and rammed us the way a destroyer rams a submarine. For one brief moment I saw the car, an old beat-up Caddy, with a terrified-looking kid at the wheel, but there was nothing I could do about it. The Caddy hit the Merc on the off-side and threw it across the freeway. My one thought as I blacked out was Judy.

I was still thinking about her when I came to the surface in a private room in the swank Jefferson Clinic paid for by Sydney Fremlin, who was sitting by my bedside crying into a silk handkerchief.

While we are on the subject of Sydney Fremlin let me give you a photo of him. He was tall, willowy with long blond hair and his age could be anything from thirty to fifty. Everyone liked Sydney: he had a warmth and a gush that overwhelm. He was artistically brilliant and had a special flair for designing way-out jewellery. His partner, Tom Luce, looked after the financial end of the business. Luce didn't know a diamond from a rock crystal, but he did know how to make a dollar breed. He and Sydney were considered rich, and being considered rich in Paradise City put them in the heavy cash bracket. Whereas Luce, fifty, portly and with a face a bulldog would envy, remained behind the scenes, Sydney fluttered around the showroom when he wasn't designing in his office. I left most of the old hens to him. They loved him, but the rich young things, the wealthy businessmen who were hunting for a special present and those who had been left granny's gems and wanted them reset or valued came to me.

Homosexuals are odd animals, but I get along with them. I have found that very often they have far more talents, more kindness, more loyalty than the average he-man I rub shoulders with in this opulent city. Of course there is the other side of the coin which can be hateful: their jealousies, their explo-

9

sive tempers, their spitefulness and their bitchiness that is always much more bitchy than any woman can hope to be. Sydney had all the assets and faults of the average homo. I liked him: we got along fine together.

With his make-up smeared with tears, his eyes pools of despair, his voice trembling, Sydney broke the news to me. Judy had died on the operating table.

I had been lucky, he told me: concussion and a nasty cut on my forehead, but in a few days, I would be as right as rain.

That was what he said: 'As right as rain.'

He talked like that. He had been to an English public school until they had booted him out for trying to seduce the sports master.

I let him sob over me, but I didn't sob over myself. Because I had fallen in love with Judy and had planned to live with her for ever and ever I had built inside myself an egg of happiness. I knew this egg had to be fragile: any real hopes of continuous happiness in this world we live in makes for a speculative egg, but I had thought and hoped that the egg would last for some time. When he told me that Judy was dead, I felt the egg go crunch and my technicoloured world turned to black and white.

In three days I was up on my feet, but I wasn't 'as right as rain'. The funeral was pretty bad. All the Country Club members turned up. Judy's mother and father came down from New York. I don't remember much about them except they seemed to me to be nice people. Judy's mother looked a lot like her daughter, and that upset me. I was glad to return to my apartment. Sydney stuck with me and I wished to God he would go away, but he sat around and maybe, looking back, he was helpful. Finally around 2200, he got to his elegant feet and said he would go home.

'Take a month off, Larry,' he said. 'Go golfing. Take a trip. Build up the pieces. You can't ever replace her, but you have your life to lead ... so take a trip and come back to us and work like hell.'

'I'll be back tomorrow and I'll work like hell,' I said. 'Thanks for everything.'

10

'I won't have you back tomorrow!' He even stamped his foot. 'I want you back in a month's time ... that's an order!'

'Balls! Work is what I want, and work is what I'm going to have! See you tomorrow.'

To me this made sense. How could I go on a golfing trip with Judy on my mind? I wouldn't give a goddamn if I went around in 110. During my brief stay in the clinic I had got it all worked out.

The egg was broken. Like Humpty Dumpty an egg is never put together again. The sooner I got back to selling diamonds the better it would be for me. I was being terribly sensible. This kind of thing happens all the time, I told myself. People who are loved, died. People who make plans, build castles in the air, even tell real estate agents they are going ahead with the purchase of a ranch house find things go wrong and their plans are blown sky high. It happens every day, I told myself. So who was I to pity myself? I had found my girl, we had made plans, now she was dead. I was thirty-eight years of age. Given reasonable luck, I had another thirty-eight years of life ahead of me. I told myself I had to pick up the pieces, get on with my job and, maybe later, find someone like Judy to marry.

At the back of my mind I knew that this was only stupid thinking. No one could ever replace Judy. She had been my chosen, and from now on any other girl would be judged by Judy's standards, and that, I knew, would give them an impossible handicap.

Anyway, I returned to the showroom with a strip of plaster to conceal the cut on my forehead. I tried to behave as if nothing had happened. Everyone tried to behave as if nothing had happened. My friends—and I had many—gave an extra squeeze when they shook hands. They were all devastatingly tactful, desperately trying to make it appear that Judy had never existed. My clients were the worst to deal with. They spoke to me in hushed voices, not looking at me, and they fell over themselves to take what I offered instead of haggling happily as they used to do.

Sydney fluttered around me. He seemed determined to keep

my mind occupied. He kept buzzing out of his office with designs, asking my opinion—something he had never done before—seemingly to hang on my words, then buzzing back out of sight, only to buzz out again in an hour or so.

The second-in-command in the showroom was Terry Melville, who had served an apprenticeship with Cartiers of London and had an impressive all-round knowledge of the jewellery trade. He was five years younger than I; a small, lean homo with long silver-dyed hair, dark blue eyes, pinched nostrils and a mouth like a knife cut. Sometime in the past, Sydney had fallen for him and had brought him to Paradise City, but now Sydney was bored with him. Terry hated me as I hated him. He hated my expertise in diamonds, and I hated him for his jealousy, his petty attempts to steal my exclusive clients and his vicious spite. He hated the fact that I wasn't a queer and, in spite of this, Sydney did so much for me. He and Sydney were always quarrelling. If it wasn't for Terry's know-how, and also, maybe, he had something on Sydney, I am sure Sydney would have got rid of him.

When I arrived a few minutes after Sam Goble, the night guard, had opened the shop Terry, who was already at his desk, came over to me.

'Sorry about it all, Larry,' he said. 'It could have been worse—you could have been dead too.'

There was that spiteful, gloating expression in his eyes that made me yearn to hit him. I could tell he was glad this had happened to me.

I nodded and, moving by him, I went to my desk. Jane Barlow, my secretary, plump, distinguished looking and pushing forty-five, came over to give me my mail. We looked at each other. The sadness in her eyes and her attempt at a smile gave me a pang. I touched her hand.

'It happens, Jane,' I said. 'Don't say anything ... there's nothing to say ... thanks for the flowers.'

With Sydney buzzing around me, the clients' hushed voices and Terry watching me malevolently from his desk, it was a hard day to take, but I took it.

Sydney wanted me to have dinner with him, but I refused. I

had to face the loneliness sooner or later, and the sooner the better. For the past two months, Judy and I always had dinner together either at my apartment or at hers; now that had come to a grinding halt. I wondered if I should go to the Country Club, but decided I couldn't face any more silent sympathy, so I bought a sandwich and sat alone in my apartment, thinking of Judy. Not a bright idea, but this first day had been hard to take. I told myself that in another three or four days my life would become adjusted ... but it didn't.

More than my egg of happiness had broken in the crash. I'm not trying to make excuses. I'm telling you what the head-shrinker finally told me. I had confidence in myself that I could ride this thing out, but there was mind damage as well as the broken egg. We didn't find this out until later, and the head-shrinker explained this mind damage did account for the way I began to behave.

There is no point in going into details. The fact was that over the next three weeks I deteriorated both mentally and physically. I began to lose interest in the things that had, up to now, been my life: my work, golf, squash, my clothes, meeting people and even money.

The most serious of them all, of course, was my work. I began to make mistakes: little slips at first, then bigger slips as the days went by. I found I didn't care if Jones wanted a platinum cigarette case with ruby initials for his new mistress. I got him the case, but forgot the initials. I forgot too that Mrs. Van Sligh had particularly requested a gold, calendar watch for her little monster of a nephew, and I sent him the gold watch without the calendar. She came into the shop like a galleon in full sail and slanged Sydney until he nearly burst into tears. This will give you just an idea the way I slipped. In three weeks I made a lot of similar mistakes: call it lack of concentration, call it what you will, but Sydney took the beating and Terry gloated.

Another thing: Judy always supervised my laundry. Now I forgot to change my shirt every day—who cares? I used to have a haircut once a week. For the first time since I can remember I now had fuzz on the nape of my neck ... who

13

cares? And so on and so on.

I quit playing golf. Who the hell, except a lunatic, I asked myself, wants to hit a little white ball into the blue and then walk after it? Squash? That was a distant memory.

Three weeks after Judy's death Sydney came out of his office to where I was sitting staring dully down at my desk and asked me if I could spare him a minute.

'Just a minute, Larry . . . no more than a minute.'

I felt a stab of conscience. I had a pile of letters and orders in my In-tray I hadn't looked at. The time was 1500, and these letters and orders had been lying in my In-tray since 0900.

'I've got mail to look at, Sydney,' I said. 'Is it important?'

'Yes.'

I got to my feet. As I did so, I looked across the showroom, where Terry was sitting behind his desk. He was watching me, a sneering little grin on his handsome face. His In-tray was empty. Whatever else he was, Terry was a worker.

I followed Sydney into his office, and he shut the door as if it were made of egg shells.

'Sit down, Larry.'

I sat down.

He began to move around his big office like a moth in search of a candle.

To help him out, I said, 'Something on your mind, Sydney?'

'*You* are on my mind.' He came to an abrupt stop and looked sorrowfully at me. 'I want you to do me a very special favour.'

'What is it?'

He began fluttering around the room again.

'For God's sake sit down!' I snapped at him. 'What is it?'

He shot to his desk and sat down. Taking out his silk handkerchief, he began to mop his face.

'What is it?' I repeated.

'It's not working out, is it, Larry?' he said, not looking at me.

'What's not working out?'

14

He put his handkerchief away, got a grip on himself, placed his elbows on the polished surface of the desk and somehow forced himself to look directly at me.

'I want you to do me a favour.'

'You said that before ... what favour?'

'I want you to see Dr. Melish.'

If he had smacked my face I couldn't have been more surprised. I reared back, staring at him.

Dr. Melish was the most expensive, most sought-after headshrinker in the city. Considering there is about one headshrinker to every fifty citizens in this city, this is saying a lot.

'What do you mean?'

'I want you to see him, Larry. I'll pick up the tab. I think you should see him.' He raised his hands as I began to protest. 'Wait a moment, Larry. Do give me time to say something.' He paused, then went on, 'Larry, you're not as right as rain. I know the ordeal you have been through. I know your dreadful loss has done damage. This I can understand. If I had been in your place I just couldn't have survived ... I know it! I think you have been marvellous coming back here and trying, but it hasn't worked. You know that, don't you, Larry?' He looked pleadingly at me. 'You do know that?'

I rubbed the back of my hand against my chin. The rasp of stubble made me stiffen. Goddamn it! I thought. I've forgotten to shave this morning! I got to my feet and crossed the room to the big wall mirror in which Sydney so often admired himself. I stared at my reflection and I felt a cold qualm. Could this mess be me? I looked at my shirt cuffs and then at my shoes that hadn't been polished for a couple of weeks.

Slowly, I returned to the chair and sat down. I looked at Sydney, who was watching me. I saw on his face his anxiety, his kindness and the tizz he was in. I wasn't so far gone that I couldn't put myself in his place. I thought of the mistakes I had made in the overflowing In-tray and how I was looking. For all the confidence I had in myself, for all the façade of bravery (can you call it that?) I just wasn't—as he put it—as right as rain.

I drew in a long, deep breath.

'Look, Sydney, let's forget Melish. I'll resign. You're right. Something has gone wrong. I'll get the hell out of here and you give Terry his chance. He's okay. Don't worry about me, because I've ceased to worry about myself.'

'You are the best diamond man in the business,' Sydney said quietly. He was now fully in control of himself, and his buzzing and fluttering had stopped. 'I'm not going to let you resign. I can't afford to lose you. You want adjustment, and Dr. Melish can fix it. Now listen to me, Larry. In the past I've done a lot of things for you, and I believe you regard me as your friend. Now is the time for you to do something for me. I want you to see Melish. I know he can straighten you out. It may take two or three months. I don't care if it takes a year. Your job with us will always be waiting for you. You are important people to me. Let me repeat: you are the best diamond man in the business. You have had a terrible knock, but it can be straightened out. This is the least you can do in return ... see Melish.'

So I saw Melish.

As Sydney had said it was the least I could do, but I had no faith in Dr. Melish until I met him. He was small, thin, balding with penetrating eyes. He had been briefed by Sydney so he knew all about my background, about Judy and how I was reacting.

Why go into details? I had three sessions with him and he finally came up with his verdict.

It came down to this: I needed a complete change of scene. I was to get away from Paradise City for at least three months.

'I understand you haven't driven a car since the accident,' he said, polishing his glasses. 'You must get a car and you must drive. The problem with you is that you imagine your loss is something unique.' He raised his hand, as I began to protest. 'I know you don't want to admit this, but all the same it is your problem. I suggest you mix with people who have bigger problems than you have. In this way, you will get your own problem in the right perspective. I have a niece who lives in Luceville. She does welfare work and she needs unpaid

16

help. I'm suggesting you should go to Luceville and work with her. I have already talked to her. I will be quite frank with you. When I told her about you she said she wasn't in the market for a disturbed person. She wants help badly, and if she has to cope with your difficulties she doesn't want you. I told her you would help her and wouldn't create any problems. It took me a little time to persuade her and now it is up to you.'

I shook my head.

'I'd be as useful to your niece as a hole in the head,' I said. 'No ... that's a dumb idea. I'll find something. Okay, I'll go away for three months. I'll ...'

He twiddled with his glasses.

'My niece needs help,' he said, staring at me. 'Don't you want to help people or have you decided people must continue to help you?'

Put like that I hadn't a come-back. What had I to lose? Sydney was going to pay me while I was trying to get rehabilitated. I should be shot of the showroom with the sympathetic hushed voices and Terry's sneering grin. Maybe this was an idea. At least it was something new, and how I yearned for something new!

Rather feebly, I said, 'But I'm not qualified for welfare work. I know nothing about it. I would be more hindrance than help.'

Melish glanced at his wrist-watch. I could see he was already thinking about his next patient.

'If my niece says she can make use of you, then she can make use of you,' he said patiently. 'Why not give it a try?'

Why not? I shrugged and said I would go to Luceville.

My first move was to buy a Buick convertible. It took an effort of will to drive it to my apartment. I was sweating and shaking by the time I had parked. I sat at the wheel for some five minutes, then forced myself to set the car in motion and I drove along the busy main street, along Seaview boulevard, back into main street and then to my apartment. When I parked this time I wasn't sweating and shaking.

Sydney came to see me off.

17

'In three months' time, Larry,' he said as he shook hands, 'you will be back and you will still be the best diamond man in the business. Good luck and God bless.'

So with a suitcase full of clothes, with no confidence in the future, I drove off to Luceville.

Dr. Melish could certainly claim credit for providing me with a change of scene.

Luceville, some five hundred miles north of Paradise City turned out to be a big straggling industrial town that dwelt under a permanent cloud of smog. Its main industry was limestone. Limestone, in case you don't know, is crushed for lime, cement and building and road materials. It happens to be Florida's main industry.

Driving slowly, it took me two days on the road to get to Luceville. I found I was now a nervous driver and every time a car swished by me I flinched, but I kept going, spending a night at a dreary motel and finally arriving at Luceville around 1100, feeling drained and jumpy.

As I approached the outskirts of the town, cement dust began to settle on my skin, making me feel unwashed and gritty. It also settled on the windshield and on the car. There was no sun. No sun, however powerful, could ever penetrate the smog and the cement dust that hung over the town. Along the highway leading to the city's centre were vast limestone factories and the noise of rock being crushed sounded like distant thunder.

I found the Bendix Hotel, recommended by Dr. Melish as the best in town, down a side street off Main Street. It was a sad affair; its glass doors were covered with cement dust, its lobby furnished with sagging bamboo chairs and its reception desk a mere counter behind which was a board with a row of keys.

A tall, overfat man with long side-whiskers dwelt behind the counter. He looked like a character who had got involved in a battle and was now licking his wounds.

He booked me in without fuss or interest. A sad-looking coloured boy took my bag and showed me to my room, over-

18

looking a tenement block and on the third floor. We travelled together in an elevator that shuddered, creaked and jerked and I was thankful to arrive in one piece.

I looked around the room. At least it had four walls, a ceiling, a toilet and shower, but there was nothing else for it to boast about.

This was certainly a change of scene.

Paradise City and Luceville were as different as a Rolls-Royce is to a third-hand, beat-up Chevvy ... maybe that is insulting the Chevvy.

I unpacked, hung my clothes in the closet, then stripped off and took a shower. Because I was determined to get to grips with myself, I put on a clean white shirt and one of my better suits. I looked at myself in the fly-blown mirror and I felt a tiny surge of confidence. At least, I thought I looked once again like someone in the executive bracket, maybe a little wan, but still, unmistakably someone with authority. It's amazing, I told myself, what an expensive, well-cut suit, a white shirt and a good tie can do for a man, even such a man as myself.

Dr. Melish had given me his niece's telephone number. Her name, he had told me, was Jenny Baxter. I called the number, but there was no reply. Slightly irritated, I prowled around the room for some five minutes, then tried again. Still no answer. I went to the open window and looked down at the street. There were a lot of people milling around : they all looked shabby, most of them dirty, most of them women, shopping. There were a lot of kids : they all looked in need of a bath. The cars that congested the streets were all covered with cement dust. I was to learn later that cement dust was the biggest enemy of this town : bigger than boredom that rated as enemy No. 2.

I called Jenny Baxter's number again, and this time a rather breathless woman's voice said, 'Hello?'

'Miss Baxter?'

'Yes.'

'I'm Laurence Carr. Your uncle, Dr. Mellish ...' I paused. She either knew about me or she didn't.

'Of course. Where are you?'

'The Bendix Hotel.'

'Will you give me about an hour? Then I'll be over.'

In spite of her breathlessness—as if she had run up six flights of stairs, which I found out later was exactly what she had done—she sounded crisp and efficient.

I wasn't in the mood to hang around in this dismal room.

'Suppose I come over?' I said.

'Oh yes . . . do that. You have the address?'

I said I had the address.

'Then come as soon as you like,' and she hung up.

I walked down the three flights of stairs. My nerves were still in a bad shape and I couldn't face the creaking elevator. I asked the coloured boy directions. He said Maddox Street was a five-minute walk from the hotel. As I had found parking for my car after a struggle, I decided to walk.

As I walked down Main Street I became aware that people were staring at me. It gradually dawned on me they were staring at my clothes. When you walk down Main Street, Paradise City, you come up against competition. You just had to be well dressed, but here, in this smog-ridden town, everyone seemed to me to be in rags.

I found Jenny Baxter in a tiny room that served as an office on the sixth floor of a shabby walk-up block. I toiled up the stairs, feeling cement dust gritty around my collar. A change of scene? Melish had certainly picked me a beauty.

Jenny Baxter was thirty-three years of age. She was tall: around five foot nine, dark with a mass of untidy black hair pinned to the top of her head and that seemed to be threatening to fall down at any moment. She was lean. By my standards, her figure was unfeminine: her breasts, unlike those of the women I knew in Paradise City, were tiny mounds and sexually uninteresting. She looked slightly starved. She was wearing a drab grey dress that she must have made herself: there could be no other explanation for its cut and the way it hung on her. Her features were good: her nose and mouth excellent, but what hooked me were her eyes. Her eyes were honest, interesting and penetrating like those of her uncle.

20

She was scribbling on a yellow form as I came into the tiny room, and she looked up and regarded me.

I stood in the doorway, unsure of myself, wondering what the hell I was doing here.

'Larry Carr?' Her voice was low toned and rich. 'Come on in.'

As I moved in, the telephone bell started up. She waved me to the only other chair, then took up the receiver. Her replies, consisting of 'yes', and 'no', were crisp and impersonal. She seemed to have the technique of cutting off what could have been a lengthy conversation had she not been able to control the speaker.

Finally, she replaced the receiver, ran her pencil through her hair and smiled at me. The moment she smiled she became a different person. It was a wonderful, open smile of warmth and friendliness.

'Sorry. This thing never stops ringing. So you want to help?'

I sat down.

'If I can.' I wondered if I really meant this.

'But not in those beautiful clothes.'

I forced a smile.

'No, but don't blame me. Your uncle didn't warn me.'

She nodded.

'My uncle is a wonderful man, but he doesn't bother with details.' She leaned back and regarded me. 'He told me about you. I believe in speaking frankly. I know about your problem, and I'm sorry about it, but it doesn't interest me, because I have hundreds of my own problems. Uncle Henry told me you want to get straightened out, but that is your problem, and in my thinking, it is up to you to straighten yourself out.' She put her hands on the soiled blotter and smiled at me. 'Please understand. In this dreadful town there is a lot of work to do and a lot of help to be given. I need help and I haven't time for sympathy.'

'I'm here to help.' I couldn't keep the resentment out of my voice. Who did she imagine she was talking to? 'What do you want me to do?'

21

'If I could only believe you really are here to help,' she said.

'I'm telling you. I'm here to help. So what do I do?'

She took from a drawer a crumpled pack of cigarettes and offered it.

I produced the gold cigarette case Sydney had given me for my last birthday. It was rather special. It had set Sydney back $1,500: a cigarette case I was proud of: call it a status symbol if you like. Even some of my clients gave it a double-take when I produced it.

'Have one of mine?' I said.

She looked at the glittering case and then at me.

'Is that really gold?'

'This?' I turned it in my hand so she could see every inch of it. 'Oh, sure.'

'But isn't it very valuable?'

The cement dust felt a little more gritty around my neck.

'It was a present ... fifteen hundred dollars.' I offered it. 'Do you want to smoke one of mine?'

'No, thank you.' She took a cigarette from her crumpled pack and dragged her eyes away from the cigarette case. 'Be careful with that,' she went on. 'It could be stolen.'

'They steal things here?'

She nodded and accepted a light from my gold lighter one of my clients had given me.

'Fifteen hundred dollars? For that amount of money I could supply ten of my families with food for a month.'

'You have ten families?' I put the cigarette case back into my hip pocket. 'Really?'

'I have two thousand five hundred and twenty-two families,' she said quietly. She opened a drawer in her battered desk and took from it a street plan of Luceville. She placed it on the desk so I could see it. The plan had been divided up into five sections with a felt pen: each section was marked from 1 to 5. 'You should know what you're walking into,' she went on. 'Let me explain.'

She went on to tell me there were five welfare workers in the town: all professionals. Each had a section of the town to

22

look after: she was in charge of the dirtest end of the stick. She glanced up and smiled. 'No one else wanted it, so I took it. I've been here for the past two years. My job is to give help when help is genuinely needed. I have a fund which is far from adequate to draw on. I visit people. I make reports. The reports have to be broken down and put on cards.' She tapped No. 5 section on the plan. 'This is my beat. It contains probably the worst of the worst in this dreadful town: close on four thousand people, including kids who are no longer kids after they are seven years old. Out here ...' Her pencil moved from the ringed section of No. 5 and tapped just beyond the town's boundary, 'is the Florida Women's House of Correction. This is a very tough prison: not only are the prisoners tough, but the conditions are tough: most of them are long term and a lot of them hopeless criminals. Up to three months ago, prison visitors weren't allowed, but I've finally convinced the people concerned that I can be helpful.' The telephone bell rang and again she went through her crisp 'yes' and 'no' routine and hung up. 'I am allowed one unpaid helper,' she went on as if the telephone conversation hadn't happened. 'People do volunteer as you have volunteered. Your job would be to keep the card index straight, take care of the telephone, handle any emergency until I can fix it, type my reports if you can read my awful handwriting. In fact, you will hold everything down until I can get back to this desk and hold it down myself.'

I shifted in the uncomfortable chair. What the hell was Melish thinking of, or didn't he know? She didn't want a man with my background, she wanted an efficient girl who could cope with office work. This was strictly no job for me.

I told her so as politely as I could, but I couldn't keep the resentment out of my voice.

'This is not a job for a girl,' Jenny said. 'My last volunteer was a retired accountant. He was sixty-five years of age with nothing to do except play golf and bridge. He jumped at the chance to help me, and he lasted two weeks. I didn't blame him when he quit.'

'You mean the job bored him?'

'No ... it didn't bore him. He became frightened.'

23

I stared at her.

'Frightened? You mean there was too much work for him to do?'

She smiled her warm smile.

'No. He was a glutton for work. He did a marvellous job while he lasted. For the first time my records were really straightened out. No ... he couldn't take what came in through that door from time to time,' and she nodded at the door of the tiny office. 'You had better know, Larry ... there is a gang of kids who terrorise this section of the city. They are known to the police as the Jinx gang. Their ages run from ten to twenty years. There are about thirty of them. The leader is Spooky Jinx—that's what he calls himself—he imagines he is a Mafia character. He is vicious and extremely dangerous and the other kids follow him slavishly. The police can't do anything about him: he's far too smart. They have picked up quite a few of the gang, but never Spooky.' She paused and then went on, 'Spooky has the idea that I am prying. He thinks I give information to the police. He thinks all the people I try to help should get on without my help. He and his gang regard their parents as creeps because they accept the hand-outs I can arrange for them: milk for the babies, clothes, coal and so on and so on and because I help them with their problems like how they can pay their rent, about their hire purchase ... all their troubles they share with me. Spooky thinks I interfere, and he makes my life difficult. Every so often they come here and try and frighten me.' Again the warm smile. 'They don't frighten me, but up to now they have succeeded in frightening my voluntary helpers.'

I listened, but I didn't believe. Some kid ... this didn't make sense to me.

'I don't think I'm quite with you,' I said. 'You mean this kid scared your accountant friend and he quit? How did this kid do that?'

'He's very persuasive. You must remember that this job is unpaid. My accountant friend explained it all to me. He is no longer young. He didn't think the job was worth the threat.'

'Threat?'

'The usual thing ... if he didn't quit they would find him one dark night. They are vicious.' She regarded me, her face suddenly grave. 'He has a wife and a nice home. He decided to quit.'

I felt a sudden tightening of my belly. I knew all about delinquent kids. Who hasn't read about them? A dark night and suddenly to be set upon by a bunch of little savages: no holds barred. A kick in the face could lose a set of decent teeth. A kick in the groin could make a man impotent.

But could such a thing happen to me?

'You don't have to volunteer,' Jenny said. She seemed to know what was going on in my mind. 'Why should you? Uncle Henry doesn't think of details. I've said that before, haven't I?'

'Let's get this straight,' I said. 'Are you telling me these kids—this Spooky—could threaten me if I worked with you?'

'Oh yes, sooner or later, he will threaten you.'

'Does his threat amount to anything?'

She crushed out her cigarette as she said, 'I'm afraid it does.'

A change of scene?

I thought for a long moment. I suddenly became aware that during this talk with this woman I hadn't once thought of Judy. This hadn't happened since the crash. Maybe a kick in the face or even in the groin would make a change.

'When do I start work?' I said.

Her warm smile enveloped me.

'Thank you ... you start as soon as you have bought yourself a sweat shirt and jeans, and please don't use that beautiful cigarette case.' She got to her feet. 'I have to go. I won't be back until four o'clock. I'll explain about the records and the card-index system then—then you are in business.'

We went down the six flights of stairs to the street and I saw her into the cement-dusty Fiat 500. She paused before starting the engine.

'Thank you for volunteering. I think we'll make out.' She regarded me for a moment through the tiny side window. 'I'm sorry about your problem. It'll come out all right ... you have to be patient,' and she drove away.

I stood on the ledge of the kerb, feeling cement dust settling over me and the humid heat turning the dust into gritty sweat. I liked her. As I stood there, I wondered what I was walking into. Did I scare easily? I didn't know. It was when the crunch came that I would know.

I walked down the narrow, noisy street to Main Street in search of a pair of jeans and a sweat shirt.

I wasn't aware when it happened, but it happened.

A dirty, ragged kid, around nine years of age, suddenly barged into me, sending me staggering. He pursed his lips and made a loud rude noise as he darted away.

It wasn't until I got back to the Bendix Hotel that I found the back of my expensive jacket had been slashed by a razor blade and my gold cigarette case gone.

TWO

After I had changed into sweat shirt and jeans, I went along to the cop house to report the loss of the cigarette case. I found, a little to my surprise, I wasn't fazed about losing it, but I knew Sydney would be devastated, and it was only fair to him to make an effort to get it back.

The charge room was thick with cement dust and the smell of unwashed feet. Sitting on a long bench against one of the walls were some ten kids: dirty, ragged and sullen. They regarded me with their small dark eyes as I walked up to the Desk Sergeant.

He was a vast hunk of human flesh with a face like a lump of raw beef. He was in shirt sleeves and sweat trickled down his face and into the creases of his thick neck, mingling with the cement dust. He was rolling a stub of pencil backwards and forwards on the blotter, and as I approached him, he raised himself slightly to break wind.

The kids on the bench giggled.

When I told him about losing the cigarette case he continued to roll the pencil backwards and forwards. Then he suddenly looked up and his pig eyes went over me with the intensity of a blow-torch.

'You a stranger here?' he asked. His voice was husky as if worn out with shouting.

I said I was a stranger here, that I had just arrived, that I was going to work with Miss Baxter, the welfare officer.

He pushed his cap to the back of his head, stared at his stub of pencil, sighed and produced a form. He told me to fill it in, then he continued to roll the pencil.

27

I filled in the form and returned it to him. Under the heading of 'Value of article stolen' I had put $1,500.

He read what I had written, then I saw his massive face tighten and pushing the form back to me, placing a dirty finger on the 'Value of article stolen' column, he demanded in his husky voice, 'What's this?'

'That's what the cigarette case is worth,' I said.

He muttered something under his breath, stared at me, then at the form.

'My jacket was slashed by a razor blade,' I said.

'That right? Your jacket worth fifteen hundred bucks too?'

'The suit cost three hundred dollars.'

He released a snorting breath down his thick nostrils.

'You got a description of the kid?'

'Around nine years of age, dark, bushy hair, black shirt and jeans,' I said.

'See him there?'

I turned and looked at the row of kids. Most of them were dark with bushy hair: most of them were wearing black shirts and jeans.

'Could be any one of them,' I said.

'Yeah.' He stared at me. 'You're sure about the value of the case?'

'I'm sure.'

'Yeah.' He rubbed the back of his sweaty neck, then put the form on the top of a pile of similar forms. 'If we find it you'll hear from us.' A pause, then, 'Staying long?'

'Two or three months.'

'With Miss Baxter?'

'That's the idea.'

He studied me for a brief moment, then a slow smile of contempt chased across his face.

'Some idea.'

'Don't you think I'll last that long?'

He sniffed, then began rolling the pencil again.

'If we find it you'll hear. Fifteen hundred bucks, huh?'

'Yes.'

He nodded, then suddenly in a voice like a clap of thunder,

28

he bawled, 'Sit still, you little bastards, or I'll get amongst you!'

I walked out, and as I reached the door I heard him say to another cop who was propping up one of the dirty walls, 'Another nutter.'

It was now twenty after 1300. I went in search of a restaurant, but there didn't seem to be any restaurants in Main Street. I finally settled for a greasy hamburger in a bar, crowded with sweaty, dirt-smelling men who looked suspiciously at me and then away.

I then took a walk. Luceville had nothing to offer except dust and poverty. I walked around the district marked on Jenny's map as section No. 5. I found myself in a world that I didn't suspect existed. After Paradise City, this seemed to me to be a trip into Dante's Inferno. I was immediately spotted as a stranger on every street. People moved away from me and some looked back and whispered about me. Kids whistled after me, and some made what is known as a loud rude noise. I walked until 1600 and then made my way back to Jenny's office. By that time I decided she must be quite a woman. To have spent two years in this hell-hole and still be able to produce that warm, friendly smile was an achievement.

I found her at the desk, scribbling on a yellow form, and she looked up and there was the warm, friendly smile.

'That's better, Larry,' she said, surveying me. 'Lots better. Sit down and I'll explain what I jokingly call my filing system. Can you handle a typewriter?'

'I can.' I sat down. I wondered if I should tell her about the cigarette case but decided not to. She had, according to her, plenty of problems without listening to mine.

We spent the next hour while she explained the system, showed me her reports and the card index and while this was going on the telephone bell rang ceaselessly.

A little after 1700 she grabbed some forms and a couple of biros and said she had to go.

'Shut up at six o'clock,' she said. 'If you could type out those three reports before you go . . .'

'Sure. Where are you off to?'

29

'The hospital. I have three old dears to visit. We open at nine in the morning. I may not be able to get in before midday. It's my day for visiting the prison. Play it by ear, Larry. Don't let them faze you. Don't let them con you either. Give them nothing but advice. If they want anything tell them you will talk it over with me.' With a wave of her hand she was gone.

I typed out the reports, broke them down and put them on cards, then filed them away. I was surprised and a little disappointed the telephone bell didn't ring: it was as if it knew Jenny wouldn't be there to answer it.

The evening lay before me. I had nothing to do except return to the hotel, so I decided I might as well stay on and get the filing system up-to-date. I have to admit I didn't do much work. When I began to read the cards I got engrossed. The cards gave me a vivid picture of crime, misery, despair and pressure for money that held me like a top-class crime novel. I began to realise what went on in section No. 5 in this smog-ridden town. When it got dark I turned on the desk light and went on reading. Time ceased to exist. I was so engrossed I didn't hear the door open. Even if I hadn't been so engrossed I still mightn't have heard it open. It was opened with stealth, inch by inch, and it was only when a shadow fell across the desk that I knew someone was in the room.

I was startled. That was, of course, the idea. With my nerves the way they were, I must have jumped six inches. I looked up, feeling my belly muscles tighten. I dropped the biro I was holding and it rolled under the desk.

I will always remember my first sight of Spooky Jinx. I didn't know it was Spooky, but after I had described him to Jenny the following morning she told me that's who it was.

Imagine a tall, very lean youth around twenty-two years of age. His shoulder-length hair was dark, matted and greasy. His thin face was the colour of cold mutton fat. His eyes, like tiny black beads, dwelt closely either side of a thin, narrow nose. His lips were loose and red and carried a jeering little smile. He wore a yellow, dirty shirt and a pair of those wayout trousers with cat's fur stuck to the thighs and around the bottoms. His lean but muscular arms were covered with tattoo designs. Across the back of each hand were obscene legends. Around his almost non-existent waist he wore a seven-inch wide belt, studded with sharp, brass nails: a terrible weapon if whipped across a face. From him came the acrid smell of dirt. I felt if he shook his head, lice would drop on to the desk.

I was surprised how quickly I got over my fright. I pushed back my chair so I could get to my feet. I found my heart was thumping, but I was in control of myself. My mind flashed back to the conversation I had with Jenny when she had warned me the kids in this district were vicious and extremely dangerous.

'Hello,' I said. 'Do you want something?'

'You the new hand?' His voice was surprisingly deep which added to his menace.

'That's right. I've just arrived. Something I can do for you?'

He eyed me over. Beyond him I saw movement and I realised he wasn't alone.

'Bring your friends in unless they are shy,' I said.

'They're fine as they are,' he said. 'You've been to the cop house, haven't you, Cheapie?'

'Cheapie? Is that you name for me?'

'That's it, Cheapie.'

'You call me Cheapie . . . I call you Smelly . . . right?'

There was a suppressed giggle in the passage which was instantly hushed. Spooky's tiny eyes lit up and became red beads.

'A wise guy . . .'

'That's it,' I said. 'Makes two of us, doesn't it, Smelly? What can I do for you?'

Slowly and deliberately, he unbuckled his belt and swung it in his hand.

'How would you like this across your stinking face, Cheapie?' he asked.

I shoved back my chair and stood up in one movement. I caught up the portable typewriter.

'How would you like this in your stinking face, Smelly?' I

31

asked.

Only a few hours ago I wondered if I would scare easily. Now I knew ... I didn't.

We regarded each other, then slowly and with the same deliberation he buckled on the belt again and I with equal slowness and with equal deliberation, put down the portable typewriter.

We seemed to be back on square A.

'Don't stay long, Cheapie,' he said. 'We don't like creeps like you. Don't go to the cops again. We don't like creeps going to the cops.' He tossed a packet done up in greasy brown paper on the desk. 'The stupid turd didn't know it was gold,' and he walked out, leaving the door open.

I stood there, listening, but they went as silently as they had come. This was a chilling experience. They seemed deliberately to move like ghosts.

I undid the packet and found my cigarette case or what was left of it. Someone had flattened it into a thin, scratched sheet of gold—probably using a sledge hammer.

That night, for the first time since Judy had died, I didn't dream of her. Instead, I dreamed of two ferret-like eyes sneering at me and a deep, threatening voice saying over and over again: Don't stay long, Cheapie.

Jenny didn't show up at the office until nearly midday. For the past hours I had been hard at work on the card index and I had got as far as letter H. The telephone rang five or six times, but each time the caller, a woman, mumbled she wanted to speak to Miss Baxter and had hung up. I had three visitors, all shabby elderly women who gaped at me, then backed away, also saying they wanted Miss Baxter. I gave them my brightest smile and asked if there was anything I could do, but they scuttled away like frightened rats. Around 1030 while I was pounding the typewriter the door slammed open and a kid I immediately recognised as the kid who had stolen my cigarette case and had slashed my jacket blew me a raspberry and then dashed away. I didn't bother to chase after him.

When Jenny arrived, her hair looking as if it would fall

down any second, her smile was less warm and her eyes worried.

'There's bad trouble at the prison,' she said. 'They wouldn't let me in. One of the prisoners went berserk. Two of the wardens have been hurt.'

'That's tough.'

She sat down and regarded me.

'Yes...' A pause, then she went on, 'Is everything under control?'

'Sure. You won't recognise your system when you have time to look at it.

'Any trouble?'

'You could call it that. I had a character here last night.' I went on to describe him. 'Mean anything to you?'

'That's Spooky Jinx.' She lifted her hands and dropped them a little helplessly into her lap. 'He's quick off the mark. He didn't bother Fred until he had been here two weeks.'

'Fred? Your accountant friend?'

She nodded.

'Tell me what happened,' she said.

I told her, but I didn't mention the cigarette case, I said Spooky had arrived and had told me not to stay long. I said we both made threatening gestures at each other, then he had left.

'I warned you, Larry. Spooky is dangerous. You had better quit.'

'How come you have remained here for two years? Hasn't he tried to run you out?'

'Of course, but he has his own odd code of honour. He doesn't attack women, and besides, I told him he couldn't scare me.'

'He can't scare me either.'

She shook her head. A strand of hair fell over her eyes. Impatiently, she pinned it back into place.

'You can't afford to be brave in this town, Larry. No ... if Spooky doesn't want you here, you have to go.'

'You don't really mean that, do you?'

'For your sake, I do. You must go. I'll manage. Don't make things more complicated than they are. Please go.'

'I'm not going. Your uncle advised a change of scene. Sorry to sound selfish, but I'm more concerned with my problem than with yours.' I smiled at her. 'Since I've arrived in this town I haven't thought of Judy. That must be good. I'm staying.'

'Larry! You could get hurt!'

'So what?' Then deliberately changing the subject, I went on, 'I had three old girls here, but they wouldn't talk to me: they wanted you.'

'Please go, Larry. I'm telling you Spooky is dangerous.'

I looked at my strap watch. It was now a quarter after midday.

'I want to eat.' I got to my feet. 'I won't be long. Is there any place in this town where I can get a decent meal? Up to now, I've been living on hamburgers.'

She regarded me, her eyes worried, then she lifted her hands in a gesture of defeat.

'Larry, I do hope you realise what you are doing and what you're walking into.'

'You said you wanted help ... that's what you're going to get. Don't let's get dramatic about it. How's about a decent restaurant?'

'All right: if that's the way you want it.' She smiled at me. 'Luigi's on 3rd Street: two blocks to your left. You can't call it good, but it isn't bad,' then the telephone bell began to ring and I left her going through her 'yes' and 'no' routine.

After an indifferent meal—the meat was tough as old leather—I went around to the cop house.

There was a solitary kid sitting on the bench against the wall. He was around twelve years of age and he had a black eye. Blood dripped from his nose on to the floor. I looked at him and he looked at me. The hate in his eyes was something to see.

I went over to the Desk Sergeant, who was still rolling his pencil backwards and forwards while he breathed heavily through his nose. He looked up.

'You again?'

'To save you trouble,' I said, not bothering to keep my voice down because I was sure the kid, sitting on the bench, was a member of Spooky's gang, 'I have my cigarette case back.' I laid the flattened strip of gold on the sergeant's blotter.

He regarded what was left of it, picked it up, turned it in his big sweaty hands, then put it down.

'Spooky Jinx returned it to me last night,' I said.

He stared down at the battered strip of gold.

I went on in a dead-pan voice, 'He said they didn't realise it was gold. You can see what they have done with it.'

He squinted at the flattened metal, then released a snort down his nose.

'Fifteen hundred bucks, huh?'

'Yes.'

'Spooky Jinx?'

'Yes.'

He sat back and pushed his cap to the back of his head. After staring at me for a long moment, his pig eyes quizzing, he asked, 'Are you making a complaint?'

'Should I?'

We stared at each other. I could almost hear his brain creak as he thought.

'Did Spooky say he had stolen your case?'

'No.'

He got some cement dust out of his left nostril with his little finger, peered at what he had found and then wiped it on his shirt front.

'You got a witness when he returned it?'

'No.'

He folded his hands together, leaned forward and regarded me with contemptuous pity.

'Listen, buster,' he said in his husky worn-out voice, 'if you plan to stay around in this goddamn town, don't make a complaint.'

'Thanks for the advice ... then I won't.' I picked up what was left of my cigarette case and dropped it into my hip-pocket. 'I thought I should report it no longer stolen.'

We looked at each other, then he said, his voice now a whisper, 'Off the record, buster, if I were you, I'd scram out of this town. Suckers who try to help Miss Baxter don't last long, and there's nothing we can do about it. Off the record, you understand?'

'Would that be one of the Jinx gang?' I asked and turned to look at the kid who was listening and watching.

'That's right.'

'He's bleeding.'

'Yeah.'

'What happened to him?'

He regarded me, his pig eyes now impersonal. I could see I was boring him.

'Why should you care, buster? If that's all you want to say, take off with the feet,' and he began to roll his pencil again.

I went over to the kid.

'I work for Miss Baxter, the welfare worker,' I said. 'It's my job to be helpful. Is there anything I can do for ...'

That was as far as I got.

The kid spat in my face.

Nothing dramatic happened for the next six days, Jenny rushed in and out, dropping yellow forms on the desk, asking anxiously if I had had trouble and then rushing out again. It baffled me that she could keep going the way she did. It also bothered me that she always wore the same drab dress and she made no effort to make the best of herself.

I typed out her reports, broke them down, put them on cards and continued to bring the card index up-to-date.

The word must have got around that I was now the official help, because the old, the lame and the halt began to come to me with their problems. Most of them tried to con me, but I took their names and addresses, wrote down a summary of their problems and told them I would talk to Jenny. Once it got into their muddled heads that they couldn't con me, they became friendly, and for the next four days, I fell for this, then discovered because of their yakking I wasn't doing any useful work, so I cut them short.

Rather to my surprise, I found I was enjoying this strange contact with a world I hadn't imagined existed. I was startled when I got a letter from Sydney Fremlin, written in purple ink, asking how I was progressing and when was I returning to Paradise City?

It was only when I read the letter that I realised I had forgotten Paradise City, Sydney and the de luxe shop with its rich, over-fed clients. There seemed to me to be no point in telling Sydney what I was doing in Luceville. Had I told him, he would have taken to his bed in despair, so I wrote that I was thinking of him (this I knew would be a sure-fire success) that I was still very nervy, that Luceville provided me with a change of scene and that I would write before long. I thought that this would keep him quiet for a week or so.

On the sixth day the scene changed.

I arrived as usual at the office around 0900. I found the office door open. A glance showed me the lock had been smashed. My careful work for the past six days: my carefully typed cards, my reports were all piled in a heap on the floor and over them had been poured melted tar. There was no question of a salvage operation: no one can deal with tar.

On the desk, printed with my red felt pen was the legend: GO HOME, CHEAPIE.

I was surprised by my reaction. The average person, I suppose, would have been angry, in despair and perhaps defeated, but I didn't react that way. I turned cold and a viciousness I had never known flowed through me. I looked at the work I had done, ruined by a stupid, vicious youth and I took up his challenge. 'You do this to me: I'll do it to you,' attitude.

It took me all the morning to clean up the mess. I worked fast, as I didn't want Jenny to know what had happened. Fortunately, this was her visiting day and she wouldn't be in until 1700. I got a can of gasoline and cleaned the tar off the floor. I walked the ruined reports and the cards down to the trash bin.

Every now and then, old women would come, and I told them I was too busy to talk to them. They gaped at the mess I was cleaning up and went away. One of them, a fat woman, pushing seventy, paused in the doorway and watched while I scrubbed the floor.

'I'll do that, Mister Larry,' she said. 'I'm more used to it

37

than you.'

Maybe the viciousness in my eyes as I looked at her scared her. She went away.

By 1600 I had cleaned it all up. I had ignored the telephone bell. I then sat down and began again on the card index.

Jenny came bustling in around 1715. She looked tired as she dropped into the straight-backed chair, facing my desk.

'Everything under control?' She sniffed. 'Gasoline? Something happen?'

'A tiny accident ... nothing,' I said. 'How did you get on?'

'All right ... the usual. People are beginning to talk about you, Larry. The oldies are getting to like you.'

'That's a step in the right direction.' I leaned back in the desk chair. 'Tell me about Spooky. Have we a card on him?'

She stiffened, staring at me.

'No. Why do you ask?'

'Have we anything on him? Where he lives?'

She continued to stare at me.

'Why do you want to know where he lives?'

I forced a casual grin.

'I've been wondering about him. I wondered, if I could contact him, if I might sell myself to him ... I mean get friendly with him. What do you think?'

Jenny shook her head.

'No ... absolutely no! No one could ever get friendly with Spooky. This is wrong thinking, Larry.' Then she paused and her eyes searched my face. 'Has something happened?'

'Happened?' I smiled at her. 'I was just wondering if I could do a rescue act ... I mean if I talked to him ... but I'll go along with what you say ... you must know ... I don't.'

'Something has happened! I know Spooky! Please tell me!'

'Nothing has happened. The trouble with you, Jenny, is you get dramatic at times.' Again I smiled at her. Then I had a sudden inspiration. 'If you haven't anything better to do, will you have dinner with me tonight?'

Her eyes widened.

'Dinner? I'd love to.'

38

It struck me from her expression this was probably her first invitation to dinner she had had since she had arrived in this godforsaken town.

'There must be some place where we can eat a decent meal. Luigi's didn't make a hit with me. Where can we go—expense no object.'

She clapped her hands.

'You really mean that—expense no object?'

'That's what I mean. I've spent nothing since I've been here and I'm loaded.'

'Then the Plaza ... it's five miles out of town. I've never been there, but I've been told about it.' She waved her hands and looked as excited as a kid.

'Okay. I'll fix it.'

She looked at her watch, then jumped to her feet.

'I must go. I have a date in five minutes.'

'Tonight then ... eight o'clock. Come to the hotel. I have a car ... okay?'

She nodded, smiled and was gone.

For some moments I sat thinking, then I dialled the cop house and asked to be connected with the Desk Sergeant. After a delay, his husky voice came over the line.

'This is Carr ... remember me?' I said.

I listened to his heavy breathing.

'Carr? Fifteen hundred bucks ... right?'

'That's it. Can you tell me where Spooky Jinx hangs out ... his pad?'

A long pause, then he said, 'What's the idea?'

'I want to contact him. He and I are due for a talk.'

'You looking for trouble, buster?'

'I'm a welfare officer—remember?' I said. 'I'm asking for information.'

Again a long pause. I could imagine him rolling his pencil backwards and forwards while he thought.

Finally, he said, 'Yeah—a welfare officer—yeah.' Another pause, then, 'His pad is 245 Lexington. The gang's meeting place is Sam's Café on 10th Street.' Another pause and more heavy breathing, then he said, 'Don't look for trouble, buster.

39

We have to clean up trouble in this town, and we don't like work.'

'That I can understand,' I said and hung up.

I got the Plaza restaurant's telephone number from the book and made a reservation for eight-forty.

But Spooky was a jump ahead of me.

Jenny arrived at the hotel at 2000. I scarcely recognised her. Her hair was in a plait and wound tightly around her beautifully shaped head. She had on a black and white dress that turned her from a frump into a desirable woman. She was obviously pleased and proud of herself as she smiled expectantly at me.

'Will I do?'

I had put on one of my better suits.

She was the first woman, since I had lost Judy, who I had taken out.

'You look wonderful,' I said and meant it.

We walked to where I had parked the Buick.

All the tyres were flat and the driving seat razor slashed. Across the windshield in big white letters was painted:

CHEAPIE GO HOME

The evening wasn't a brilliant success. How could it have been? Jenny was upset about the car, although I played it cool, damping down my blazing hatred of Spooky Jinx. I took her back to the hotel, sat her in one of the sagging bamboo chairs while I telephoned Hertz Rent-a-Car. In fifteen minutes a car was delivered. While we waited, I tried to soothe Jenny down.

'Look, this doesn't matter,' I said. 'I'll get the car fixed ... that's no problem. Forget it as I'm forgetting it.'

'But, Larry, don't you see this dreadful boy won't leave you alone until you have gone? You must go! He could hurt you! Please ... I know him. He's vicious! He won't stop at anything. He ...'

'Jenny!' The snap in my voice stopped her short. 'You and I are having dinner together. Let's skip Spooky. Let's talk about each other. You look marvellous. Why do you always

40

wear that awful grey dress?'

She stared at me, then shrugged helplessly.

'Oh, that? Look at the people in this town. It's my disguise. That's why I asked you to wear a sweat shirt and jeans. You have to dress the part here.'

'Yes.' I saw her point, then I went on, 'I have only been here eight days, but I'm getting the photo. Do you really think you can help these people? No, wait a minute ... I tell you I'm getting the photo. These people are scroungers. They try all the time to con. They take. Is it such a hot idea to work at the pressure you work? Aren't you rushing up a moving staircase that is going the wrong way?'

She thought about this, then said quietly, 'Someone has to do it. One out of fifty really needs help. If I can help that one, then I'm doing a job.'

The Hertz car arrived. I signed the form and we drove out of the town.

The Plaza restaurant, on the side of a hill with a view of the lights of Luceville, was plush and expensive. The food was good. There was a band that played soft swing. It was crowded with bulky elderly men and fat, bulging women: all who talked at the top of their voices: the kind of scene Paradise City specialises in.

We ate, made conversation, but it wasn't a success because we were both thinking of the ruined car, Spooky and the drab, sordid life that was the background of Luceville, but we kept these thoughts to ourselves.

I drove Jenny back to her apartment. By this time it was 2300.

She thanked me for a lovely evening. The expression in her eyes told me how worried she was.

'Larry ... please be sensible. Please go back to your own home.'

'I'll think about it. Let's do this again.' I touched her hand. 'Next time we will have real fun,' and I left her and drove back to the hotel.

I changed into the sweat shirt and jeans, then I went down to the lobby and asked the sad coloured boy where I could find

41

10th Street. He looked at me as if I were crazy. Then when I asked him again, he said it was a good half-hour's walk. He began to give directions, but I told him to skip it.

I went out into the hot, cement-dusty night and got a taxi. I arrived at the top of 10th Street at 2335. I paid off the taxi and started down the dimly lit street, which was lined with trash bins that smelt as if each one of them contained a rotting corpse.

People milled around: most of them were old drunks, old women ... people without a roof. Further down the street, the scene changed. Neon lights made harsh white pools on the filthy sidewalk. I now moved in the shadows. There were the usual Honky Tonk parlours, the strip-tease clubs, blue movie shows, the bars and the cafés. This part of the street was inhabited by the young. Boys with long hair, girls with hot pants and see-through, milled aimlessly around and created noise. Most of them carried transistors which exploded into ear-shattering noise of pop.

Further down the street I saw a flashing sign that spelt out:

SAM'S CAFE

Still keeping in the shadows, I walked past the café.

Outside, in an orderly rank were eight Honda motorcycles: flashy, powerful with crash helmets hanging from the handlebars. The café was crowded. I had a glimpse of young people wearing the usual uniform young people dig for, and the noise erupting from the café was deafening.

I walked to the end of the street, turned and walked back. I found a dark, smelly doorway and I stepped into darkness. From there I could see the café. I leaned against the wall and waited. My smouldering rage against Spooky was now like a forest fire inside me. I thought of the cards, ruined by tar, and my car.

Around midnight, there was an exodus from the café. Kids spilled out, shouting and screaming and went running off down the street. Then eight thin youths came swaggering out: lead-

42

ing them was Spooky. All of them were wearing the same uniform: yellow shirts and cat's fur pants and a wide nail-studded belt. They got astride their Hondas, slapped on their helmets, and then the air was split with the fiendish sound of powerful engines revving and revving. Then they shot off. The noise they made sounded as if the third world war had begun.

I memorised the number of Spooky's bike, then I walked to the end of the street, picked up a taxi after a wait and returned to the hotel. I stretched out on the uncomfortable bed and waited. While I waited, I smoked innumerable cigarettes and let the forest fire of my hate rage, then around 0300, I got off the bed and went silently down the stairs to the hotel lobby.

The nightman was fast asleep. I let myself out into the hot cement-dusty street and went in search of a taxi. Eventually, I found one on a rank in Main Street, the driver dozing.

I told him to take me to Lexington. It was a ten-minute drive. Luceville was asleep. There were no cars to stop a fast run.

The driver pulled up at the top of the street.

'Stick around,' I said. 'I'll be back.'

It was the kind of street where vermin must breed. Either side, tenement blocks with old-fashioned iron fire-escapes blotted out the sky. Stinking trash bins, newspapers scattering the sidewalk, used contraceptives and used sanitary towels lay in the gutters.

I walked down the deserted, silent street until I came to the tenement block that had a plaque: No. 245: Spooky's pad. I paused, seeing the glittering Honda motorcycle at the kerb. I checked the number plate. Here was Spooky's pride and joy.

I looked up and down the deserted street, making sure there would be no witness. The only witness was a lean, mangy cat that darted from the shadows into an alley.

I turned the Honda on its side, then I unscrewed the gas cap. When the gasoline had made a big puddle around the bike, I struck a match, stepped back and tossed the burning match into the puddle.

THREE

The following morning, on my way to the office, I called in on a hardware store and bought a pick-axe handle. I took it to the office and put it by the side of my desk, out of sight, but where I could get it with one swift movement. I had an idea I might need it.

Jenny came bustling in around 1000, the usual yellow forms clutched in her hand and wearing the drab grey dress. I found it hard to recognise the same woman I had taken out to dinner last night.

She thanked me again for the dinner, asked if I had slept well, to which I said I had slept fine: a lie, of course, as I had hardly slept at all. She peered at what I was doing and from the expression on her face I could tell she was surprised I was only at letter C. She wasn't to know that Spooky had ruined the work I had done, and I wasn't going to tell her. Then she took off.

I thumped the typewriter and kept my ears cocked.

Around 1100 Spooky arrived with seven of his buddies, so silently that, in spite of listening all the time, in spite of expecting him, I was taken unawares.

If he hadn't been a sadistic show-off he would have had me cold. Probably he felt completely secure with seven of his hulking buddies behind him.

He stood before my desk and looked gloatingly at me: his tiny eyes red buttons of vicious hate.

Slowly, he began to undo his belt.

'This, Cheapie, is the payoff . . .'

But by this time I had absorbed the shock of seeing him and

44

I acted.

Had he walked in, his belt swinging, he would have nailed me, but he wanted to see me cringe.

I stood up, kicked away my chair, grabbed the pick-axe handle and hit him all in one swift movement.

I didn't give a goddamn if I killed him. I hit him with all the strength of my two arms and with all the weight of my body. My viciousness matched his.

The pick-axe handle caught him on the side of his face. Two of his front teeth flew out and landed on my desk. Blood spurted from his nose. His jaw went slack and hung. He fell, his eyes rolling back and he lay in a crumpled, smelly heap on the floor.

I didn't even pause to look at him. I came around the desk like a rampaging bull, the blood-stained pick-axe handle flaying.

His seven buddies scattered into the passage. I hit out right and left. I was demented with vicious rage. They ran, falling over each other to get down the stairs. I went after them, hammering their cowering backs to the second landing.

Then I paused while they continued pounding down the next flight, like the frightened rats they were.

Faces appeared at doorways. People gaped at me as I went up the stairs and back into the office.

I hated to touch him, but I wanted him out of here. I grabbed hold of his filthy, greasy hair and dragged his unconscious body along the passage and to the stairs. Then I booted him and he rolled over and over to land with a crash on the lower landing. He lay there, blood running from his nose: as broken as anyone could be broken.

I returned to the office, put the pick-axe handle in one of the closets, then called the cop house.

I asked for the Desk Sergeant.

'This is Carr ... remember me? Fifteen hundred bucks?'

I listened to his heavy breathing while be absorbed this information.

'What's on your mind this time?' he finally asked.

'Spooky looked in,' I said. 'He wanted to alter the shape of my face with his nail-studded belt. I had to get a little rough with him. I suggest you send an ambulance ... he seems in urgent need of care and attention,' and I hung up.

For a few moments I sat still, taking stock of myself. I looked at my hands, lying on the blotter. There was no shake. I felt completely relaxed as if I had had a good round of golf, and this puzzled me. The whole violent affair had taken two minutes. I had done something that, three weeks ago, even less, I would have thought impossible. I had faced eight thugs, maimed one and had driven the others away. And now it was over I felt no sense of shock. All I wanted was a cigarette which I lit. Then, knowing Jenny would be along in an hour or so I got some cleaning rags from the closet and cleaned up Spooky's blood. As I was dropping the rags into the trash basket I heard an ambulance siren.

I didn't bother to go out into the passage. I sat at my type-writer and continued to work on the card index.

After a while two cops came in. 'What's going on?' one of them asked. 'What's all this about?'

Both of them were grinning and looked happy.

'Spooky came here, got rough, so I got rough,' I said.

'Yeah ... we've seen him. Come on, buddy, the Sarg wants to talk to you.'

As they drove me to the cop house they told me the latest ball scores they had heard over the radio. For cops, they were more than friendly.

I walked up to the Desk Sergeant, who was rolling his pen-cil, but this time, his heart didn't seem to be in it.

He squinted at me with his pig eyes, sniffed, scratched under his right armpit, then said, 'Let's have it. What hap-pened?'

'I told you over the telephone, Sergeant,' I said. 'Spooky arrived with seven of his pals. He threatened me. I threw him out and his pals took off. That's it.'

He studied me, pushed his cap to the back of his head and released a snorting grunt.

'Just got the medical report,' he said. 'The punk has a bust jaw, a bust snout, eight teeth missing and he's lucky to be alive.' He peered at me. 'What did you hit him with—a brick?'

'In his hurry to leave, he fell down the stairs,' I said woodenly.

He nodded.

'Sort of fell over his feet, huh?'

'Sort of.'

A long pause, then I said, 'Have you seen his belt? It has sharpened nails. He was proposing to whip my face with it.'

He nodded again while he continued to regard me.

'Should we cry over him, Sergeant?' I went on. 'If you think I should, I could send him some flowers ... if you think I should.'

He began rolling his pencil again.

'He could make a complaint ... assault. We would have to investigate.'

'Suppose we wait until he does?'

Again the pig eyes examined me, then he stopped rolling his pencil.

'Yeah ... that's an idea.' He looked past me and surveyed the empty charge room. For some reason or other no one at this moment was in trouble and we were alone. He leaned forward and said in his husky voice, 'Every officer in this town has been wanting to do what you did to that sonofabitch.' His raw beef of a face split into a wide, friendly grin. 'But watch it, Mr. Carr. Spooky is like the elephant: he won't forget.'

'I have work to do,' I said, still keeping my face wooden, but feeling an inward surge of triumph. 'Can I get back to it?'

'Oh, sure.' He sat back and now his eyes were thoughtful. 'A taxi driver reported he saw a motorbike go up in flames last night ... Spooky's bike. Would you know anything about it?'

'Should I?'

He nodded.

'That's the correct answer, but don't lean on it, Mr. Carr. We have to keep law and order in this town.'

'When you can spare a minute, Sergeant,' I said, 'you might mention that to Spooky.'

We looked at each other and then I left.

When I got back to the office I found Jenny there. Of course she had heard all about it. This was something I couldn't hope to keep quiet. She was white and shaking.

'You could have killed him!' she exclaimed. 'What did you do to him?'

'He got rough ... I got rough.' I went around the desk and sat down. 'He had it coming. I've seen the police, They are as happy as kids at a party. So let's forget Spooky.'

'No!' Anger I hadn't expected ever to see jumped into her eyes. 'You think you're a hero, don't you? You're not! I know you destroyed his motorbike! You've broken his nose and his jaw! You're as brutal and as vicious as he is! I can't have you here! You're spoiling everything I'm trying to do! I want you to go.'

I stared at her.

'You'll be telling me next you're going to the hospital to hold his hand.'

'There is no need to make a cheap remark. I want you to go!'

I began to get angry, but I controlled my temper.

'Look, Jenny, you must face facts. Thugs like Spooky have to be treated like the animals they are,' I said. 'Suppose I had sat still and let him whip the flesh off my face with his belt. Would that have put me right with you?'

'You nearly killed him! Don't talk to me! Get up and go!'

'Okay.' I got to my feet and walked around the desk. 'I'll be at the hotel for a few more days.' I reached the door, paused and looked at her. 'Jenny, the trouble with nice people is they are seldom realistic. Spooky is a savage animal. Okay ... go ahead and hold his hand if that's the way you feel. Everyone is entitled to their way of thinking, but be careful. There is no animal yet born more dangerous and more savage than Spooky.'

'I won't listen to you!' Her voice rose. 'My uncle made a mistake sending you here! You are quite unsuitable for welfare work! You can't nor ever will realise that people do react to kindness! I've worked here for two years and you have been here ten days. You ...'

So then I let my temper have a free hand.

'Wait!' The snap in my voice startled her and cut her short. 'What have you done with your kindness in two years? People don't appreciate kindness! All they want from you is a meal ticket or a hand-out. They would accept a handout if you threw it at them! All these women who come pestering you are scroungers. Are you sure they aren't laughing at you? This sector of yours has been terrorised by Spooky for years. Even the police couldn't handle him. Well, I've handled him and maybe you'll find I've done more for this sector of your town in ten days than you have done in two years!'

'Go away!'

I saw I had hurt her, but I didn't care. I had done something no one had had the guts to do in this miserable town: I had fixed Spooky Jinx and had fixed him good.

I left her and walked back to the Bendix Hotel.

On the way I became aware people didn't edge away from me: some of them even smiled at me. News travels fast. A cop, resting his feet on the edge of the kerb, gave me a friendly wink.

I had suddenly become popular in Luceville, but I didn't feel ten feet tall: Jenny had spoilt my triumph. I just couldn't see how she could be so stupid.

I wondered what I was going to do. Maybe, in a day or so she would have cooled off and we could get together again. Paradise City seemed a long way off. I didn't want to go back there—anyway just yet.

I found I was hungry so I went to Luigi's restaurant. The two old waiters beamed on me. On my first visit they had ignored me. A fat, elderly man with food stains on his suit came over as I was eating. He said his name was Herb Lessing.

'I run the Drug store around the corner. I wanted you to know I think you did a fine job, Mr. Carr. That bastard had it coming. Now, maybe I can rest at night.' He paused, breathed over me, then added, 'I reckon you've done a real service to this town.'

I wondered what Jenny would have said had she heard this. I nodded, thanked him and went on eating. He regarded me with open admiration and then returned to his table.

After lunch and because I couldn't face the hotel and had nothing to do, I went to a movie. It didn't hold me as I kept thinking of Jenny.

I walked back to the hotel, taking my time and went up to my room.

You're as brutal and as vicious as he is!

I lit a cigarette, then laid on the bed and thought about what she had said.

I finally decided she could be right. Something must have happened to me. I recalled the demented rage that had seized hold of me as I had hit Spooky and then had turned on his buddies. Admittedly I had been provoked, but I knew, three months ago, I would never have acted like this. Was this demented outburst of rage due to the crash? Had one of my mental cogs been jogged out of place? Should I consult Dr. Melish? Then I decided I couldn't be bothered. For the first time, since I had lost Judy, I felt an over-powering urge for a woman.

What the hell was happening to me? I asked myself. Maybe it would be an idea to visit the local whorehouse—in a town like Luceville, there must be a whorehouse. The reception clerk would know.

I looked at my watch: the time was 1815. As I swung off the bed, I told myself I would have a woman, have a good dinner at the Plaza and then let tomorrow take care of itself.

As I was leaving the room the telephone bell rang. I didn't know as I picked up the receiver this was to alter my whole way of life.

'Mr. Carr? This is O'Halloran ... Desk Sergeant, city police.'

I recognised the husky, worn-out voice.

'Yes, Sergeant?'

'Been trying to find you, then remembered you're checked in at the Bendix.'

'Yes?' I was now very alert, all thoughts of having a woman

gone, and I felt my belly muscles tighten. 'Something wrong?'

'Yeah ... you could say that.' He snorted, then went on, 'Miss Baxter fell down stairs. She's hospitalised.'

I felt my heart beat slow.

'Is she badly hurt?'

'Well, nothing serious, but bad.' He paused to snort again, then went on, 'Broken wrist, broken ankle, fractured collar-bone ... quite a fall.'

'Where is she?'

'City hospital. Thought you should know.'

'Thanks,' I said.

I heard a sound that puzzled me. Could he be rolling his pencil?

'There was a trip wire at the head of the stairs,' he said. 'Off the record, I figure it was meant for you, but she fell over it.'

A smouldering fire of rage began inside me.

'Is that right?' I said and I hung up.

For a long moment I stared bleakly at the opposite wall. The trip wire was meant for me. With all her cock-eyed ideas of kindness, Jenny had taken a fall that could have killed her.

I called the reception clerk, and asked him to connect me with the city hospital. When I got through, I asked if I could see Miss Baxter. Some nurse said not until tomorrow. Miss Baxter was under sedation. I thanked her and hung up.

It was getting dark now and the shadows were closing in, I walked from the hotel to Jenny's office and climbed the six flights of stairs. The rage inside me grew and grew. I still had the key I had forgotten to give her when I had walked out. I unlocked the door, turned on the light, went to the closet and took out the pick-axe handle. I laid it down by the side of my desk, out of sight. All the other one-room offices in the building were closed: no lights showed except the light from my window. I hoped this would entice Spooky's buddies to come up and take care of me. It was a bait I longed for them to take so I could get amongst them and do them damage, but they didn't come.

I sat there, waiting until 2330, then carrying the pick-axe handle, I shut the office and walked down to the street. I found a taxi and told the driver to take me to 10th Street.

When we arrived, I paid him off and waited until he had driven away. I walked down the street, which, at this hour, was deserted although the strip-tease clubs, and the cafés were doing business. I arrived outside Sam's Café. Parked in a neat row were seven gleaming Honda motorcycles. The noise erupting from the café was deafening. Holding the pick-axe handle under my arm, ready for action, I took off the caps of the bikes. Then I turned the bikes on their sides so the gas spilled out.

A girl in a mini skirt and a boy with beads around his neck came out of the café. They stopped to stare at what I was doing.

'Hi!' The boy said weakly. 'Leave those bikes alone!'

I ignored him. Stepping away, I lit a cigarette.

The girl let out a scream like the bleat of a sheep. The boy bolted into the café.

I moved back, then flicked the lighted cigarette into the pool of gasoline.

There was a bang, a blinding flash and then flames. The heat forced me to retreat across the road to the far sidewalk.

Seven youths in their dirty yellow shirts and their cat's-fur pants came spilling out of the café, but the heat brought them to a standstill. I watched. None of them had the guts to pull even one of the bikes out of the now roaring furnace. They just stood there, watching the Hondas, which were probably their only love, melt in the flames.

I waited, both hands gripping the pick-axe handle, willing them to come at me so I could smash them, but they didn't. Like the stupid stinking sheep that they were, they stood, watching the destruction of the toys that had made them feel like men, and did nothing about it.

After five minutes I got bored and walked away.

Although Jenny in her bed of pain didn't know it, I felt I had made the score even.

I slept dreamlessly until 0810 when the telephone bell woke me.

I picked up the receiver.

'Mr. Carr ... there's a police officer asking for you,' the reception clerk said, reproach in his voice.

'I'll be down,' I said. 'Ask him to wait.'

I didn't hurry. I shaved and showered and put on one of my expensive sports shirts and a pair of whipcord slacks, then I went down in the creaky elevator.

Sergeant O'Halloran, massive, in shirt sleeves with his cap at the back of his head, filled one of the bamboo chairs. He was smoking a cigar and reading the local newspaper.

I went over and sat by his side.

'Morning, Sergeant,' I said. 'Have a coffee with me?'

He put down his newspaper and, folding it carefully, placed it on the floor.

'I'm on duty in half an hour,' he said in his husky worn-out voice, 'but I thought I'd drop by. Never mind the coffee.' He stared at me with his pig eyes that were ice cold and diamond hard. 'There was a hell of a fire on 10th Street last night.'

'Is that right?' I stared back at him. 'I haven't seen the papers yet.'

'Seven valuable motorbikes were destroyed.'

'Someone put in a complaint?'

He crossed one thick leg over the other.

'Not yet, but they could.'

'Then of course you will have to investigate.'

He leaned forward and there was a touch of red in his pig eyes.

'I'm getting worried about you, Carr. You are the coldest, most ruthless sonofabitch that has arrived in this town. Off the record, I'm telling you something: you pull one more trick like this and you're in trouble. You nearly set the whole goddamn street on fire. It's got to stop.'

I wasn't intimidated.

'Produce your witnesses, Sergeant, and I will then accept trouble, but not before. I'm not admitting anything, but it seems to me the police in this town can't cope with bastards like Spooky Jinx and his kind, so I don't see why you should set up a bleat when someone does.' I got to my feet. 'If you want a cup of coffee, join me. I do.'

He sat there, turning his half-smoked cigar around in his thick fingers as he stared at me.

'I'm telling you ... lay off. Just one more trick from you and you're in the tank. You're lucky I dig for Miss Baxter. She's doing a swell job in this town. Maybe you think you're levelling the score, but enough's enough. I went along with what you did with Spooky. He had it coming, but this job last night I don't dig for.' He heaved himself to his feet and faced me. 'I'm getting a feeling about you. I'm getting the idea you could be more tricky than this gang of stupid bastard kids. If I'm right, then you could be heading for trouble.'

'You said that before,' I said politely. 'Did you say this was off the record?'

'Yeah.'

'Then still off the record, Sergeant, go get screwed.' I walked across the dreary lobby into the even more dreary breakfast room. I drank a cup of bad coffee, smoked and read the local rag. The picture of the seven moronic-looking youths, wet-eyed and mourning their vanished Hondas, gave me a feeling of intense satisfaction.

Around 1000 I left the hotel and walked to the only florist in the town. I bought a bunch of red roses, then walked to the city hospital. On the way, I met people who smiled at me and I smiled back.

Eventually, after a long wait, I arrived at Jenny's bedside. She was looking pale and her long hair was done in plaits and lay either side of her shoulders.

A nurse fussed around with a vase for the flowers and then went away. While she was fussing I looked down at Jenny, feeling ten feet tall. She wasn't to know that I had evened the score. I had not only fixed Spooky but I had now dismounted his seven moronic buddies: dismounting them, destroying their Hondas was, to them, having their genitals cut off.

'Hi, Jenny, how goes it?' I asked.

She smiled ruefully.

'I didn't expect to see you. After the way I talked to you I thought we were through.'

I pulled up a chair and sat down.

'You don't get rid of me that easily. Forget it. How do you feel?'

'I can't forget it. I'm sorry I said you didn't know kindness. I was angry, and I guess some women, when they are angry, say things they don't always mean. Thank you for the roses ... they're lovely.'

I wondered what she would think when she heard about the seven destroyed Hondas.

'Forget it,' I said. 'You haven't told me how you feel.'

She made a little grimace.

'Oh, all right. The doctor says I'll be around again in three or four weeks.'

'They fixed that trip wire for me. I'm sorry you had to walk into it.'

There was a long pause as we looked at each other.

'Larry ... if you feel you can, you could be helpful,' she said. 'You don't have to worry about the office: that's been taken care of. The City Hall has sent a replacement, but there is a special case ... would you handle it for me?'

A special case.

I should have told her I was through with this welfare racket. I should have told her the racket was strictly for suckers, but my destiny nudged me.

'Sure ... What is it?'

'Tomorrow, at eleven o'clock, a woman is being released from prison. I've been visiting her. I made her a promise.' Jenny paused to look at me. 'I hope you will understand, Larry, that to people in prison, a promise means a lot. I promised her I would meet her when she came out and I would drive her home. She has been in prison for four years. This will be her first experience of liberty, and I just don't want to let her down. If I'm not there ... if nobody is there, it could undo all the work I've done on her ... so would you meet her, tell her what's happened to me and why I couldn't keep my promise, be nice to her and take her to her home?'

Jesus! I thought, how can anyone be so simple-minded! A woman who has been locked up in a tough prison for four years just had to be tougher than steel. Like all the other women who scrounged on Jenny, this woman was taking her for a ride, but because it was due to me that Jenny had a broken ankle, a broken wrist and a fractured collar-bone, I decided I would go along with her.

'That's no problem, Jenny. Of course I'll be there.'

I got her warm, friendly smile.

'Thank you, Larry ... you'll be doing a real kindness.'

'So how do I know her?'

'She will be the only one released at eleven o'clock. She has red hair.'

'That makes it easy. Why is she in prison ... or shouldn't I ask?'

'No, you shouldn't ask. It doesn't matter, does it? She's served her sentence ...'

'Yes. So where do I take her?'

'She has a place off Highway three. Her brother lives there. She'll give you directions.'

The nurse came fussing in and said Jenny must rest. She was probably right. Jenny looked drained out.

'Don't worry about anything.' I got to my feet. 'I'll be there at eleven o'clock. You haven't told me her name.'

'Rhea Morgan.'

'Okay. I'll see you tomorrow afternoon and tell you how it went.'

The nurse shooed me out.

As I walked away from the hospital, I realised I had most of the day ahead of me with nothing to do. Although I didn't know it then, by tomorrow at eleven o'clock, when I met Rhea Morgan, the scene would change.

At 1104 the grille guarding the entrance to the Women's House of Correction swung open and Rhea Morgan walked into the pale sunshine that struggled with the smog and the cement dust.

I had been sitting in the Buick which I had had fixed, for some twenty minutes and seeing her, I flicked away my cigarette, got out of the car and went over to her.

It is difficult to give a description of this woman except to say she had thick hair, the colour of a ripe chestnut and she was tall, slim and dressed in a shabby black dustcoat, dark blue slacks and her shoes were dusty and scuffed. There are beautiful women, pretty women and attractive women, but Rhea Morgan didn't fall into any of these categories. She was strictly Rhea Morgan. She had good features: a good figure, long legs and square shoulders. Her extraordinary deep green eyes made an impact on me. They were big eyes, and they regarded the world with suspicion, cynical amusement blatant sexuality. This was a woman who had done everything. As we regarded each other, I had a feeling she was years older in experience than I was.

'I'm Larry Carr,' I said. 'Jenny is in hospital. She's had an accident. She asked me to fill in for her.'

She regarded me. Her eyes took off my clothes and studied my naked body. This was something I had never experienced before. I reacted to her slow examination as any man would react.

'Okay.' She looked at the Buick. 'Let's get out of here. Give me a cigarette.'

She had a low, husky voice as dead-pan as her green eyes.

As I offered my pack of cigarettes, I said, 'Don't you want to know how badly hurt Jenny is?'

'Give me a light.'

Anger surged up in me as I lit her cigarette.

'Did you hear what I said?'

She dragged smoke down into her lungs and expelled it, letting it drift down her thin nostrils and out of her hard mouth.

'Is she?'

The indifference in her voice told me as nothing else could tell me what a sucker Jenny was.

'A broken ankle, a broken wrist and a fractured collar-bone,' I said.

She took another drag at the cigarette.

'Do we have to stick around here? I want to go home. That's your job, isn't it ... to take me home?'

She moved around me and walked to the Buick, opened the

57

off-side door, slid in and slammed the door shut.

Cold rage gripped me. I jerked open the car door.

'Come on out, you bitch!' I yelled at her. 'You can walk! I'm not a sucker like Jenny! Come on out, or I'll drag you out!'

She took another drag at the cigarette as she eyed me.

'I didn't think you were. Don't get your bowels in an uproar. I pay off. Take me home and I'll pay the fare.'

We looked at each other. Then this sexual urge I had had the previous evening took hold of me. It was as much as I could do to restrain the urge to drag her out of the car and lay her on the dirty, cement-dusty road.

The emerald eyes were now pools of promise.

I slammed the door shut, walked around the car and got in under the steering wheel.

I drove fast down to Highway 3.

While I waited to edge the car into the fast traffic at the intersection, she said, 'How come you got mixed up with that little dope? You seem to talk my language.'

'Just keep your mouth shut. The more I hear from you the less I like you.'

She laughed.

'Man! You really are my thing!'

She dropped questing fingers on my lap. I threw her hand off.

'Shut up and stay still or you'll walk,' I snarled at her.

'Okay. Give me another cigarette.'

I flicked my pack at her and started along the highway. Five minutes of fast driving brought us past the Plaza restaurant.

'So that still exists,' she said.

I suddenly realised this woman had been locked away for four years. This thought gave me a jolt. I eased up on the gas pedal.

'Where do I take you?' I asked, not looking at her.

'A mile ahead and the first sign post to your left.'

Following her directions, a mile ahead, I swung the car off the highway and on to a dirt road.

I glanced at her from time to time. She sat away from me,

smoking, staring through the windshield: in profile, her face looked as if it had been cut out of marble: as cold and as hard.

I thought of what she had said: *I'll pay for my fare.* Did she mean what I thought she meant? My desire for sex sent wave after wave of hot blood through me. I couldn't remember ever having this violent feeling before and it shook me.

'How much further?' I asked huskily.

'Turn left at the end of the road and there we are,' she said and flicked the butt of her cigarette out of the open window.

It was another mile up the road, then I turned left. A narrow lane faced me and I slowed the Buick. Ahead of me I could see a clap-board bungalow that looked lost, broken and sordid.

'Is this your home?'

'That's it.'

I pulled up and regarded the building. To me, there could be no worse place in which to live. Tangled weeds, some of them five feet high surrounded the bungalow. The fencing had gone, smothered in weeds; several oil drums, empty food cans and bits of paper lay scattered around the approach to the bungalow.

'Come on!' she said impatiently. 'What are you gaping at?'

'Is this really your home?'

She lit another cigarette.

'My stupid punk of a father lived here. This is all he left us,' she said. 'Why should you care? If you don't want to go further, I can walk the rest of the way.'

'Us? Who is us?'

'My brother and me.' She opened the car door and slid out. 'So long, Mr. Do-gooder. Thanks for the ride,' and she started over the rough, debris-strewn ground with long, quick strides.

I waited until she had reached the front door, then set the car in motion, pulled up when the road petered out and leaving the car, walked up to the bungalow.

The front door stood open. I looked into the tiny lobby. A door to my left stood open.

I heard a man say, 'Jesus! So you're back!'

59

A wave of cold, bitter frustration ran through me. *I'll pay my fare*, had been a con.

I moved forward, and Rhea, hearing me, turned.

We stared at each other.

'You want something?' she asked.

A man appeared. He had to be her brother: tall, powerfully built with the same thick chestnut-coloured hair, a square-shaped face, green eyes. He was in something that looked like a dirty sack and soiled jeans. He would be some years younger than she: twenty-four, probably less.

'Who's this?'

'I'm Larry Carr,' I said. 'A welfare worker.'

We regarded each other and I began to hate him as he gave a sneering little chortle.

'The things that go with you,' he said to Rhea. 'Maggots out of cheese ... now a welfare worker!'

'Oh, shut up!' she snapped. 'He's a do-gooder. Any food in this stinking place?'

I looked from one to the other. They were right out of my world. My mind flashed back to Paradise City with its fat, rich old women and their dogs, Sydney, buzzing and fluttering, the clean, sexy looking kids in their way-out gear, and yet this sordid scene had a fascination for me.

'How about having a wash?' I said. 'I'll buy you both a meal.'

The man shoved Rhea aside and moved up to me.

'You think I need a wash?'

Then I really hated him.

'Sure you certainly do ... you stink.'

Watching, Rhea laughed and moved between us.

'He's my thing, Fel. Leave him alone.'

Over her shoulder, the man glared at me, his green eyes glittering. I waited for his first move. I felt the urge to hit him. He might have seen this in my expression for he turned and walked across the shabby, dirty room, pushed open a door and disappeared.

'Some home-coming,' I said. 'Do you want me to buy you a meal?'

She studied me. Her emerald-green eyes were jeering.

'Man! Don't you want it!' she said. 'When you have me, it'll cost you more than a meal.'

This was a challenge and a promise and I grinned at her.

'I'm at the Bendix Hotel ... anytime,' I said and walked out of the bungalow and to my car.

Sooner or later, I told myself, we would come together: it would be an experience worth waiting for.

I drove back to Luceville, had lunch at Luigi's, then bought a bunch of grapes and went to the hospital.

Jenny was looking brighter. She smiled eagerly as I sat on the hard-backed chair by her bedside.

'How did it go?' she asked, after thanking me for the grapes.

I gave her an edited version of my meeting with Rhea Morgan. I said I had met her, and driven her to her home and had left her there. I said her brother seemed tricky and hadn't welcomed me.

But Jenny wasn't that easy to fool. She looked searchingly at me.

'What do you think of her, Larry?'

I shrugged.

'Tough.' I tried to give the impression that as far as I was concerned, Rhea meant nothing to me. 'I told her you had an accident and I was filling in.'

She smiled her warm smile.

'She didn't care, did she?'

'No ... she didn't care.'

'You're still not right, Larry. People do react to kindness.'

'She doesn't.'

'Yes, that's right, but a lot of people do, but of course, some don't. She is a difficult case.'

'You can say that again.'

A long pause as we looked at each other, then she said, 'What are you going to do? You won't stay on here, will you?'

'Tell me something. You've been in hospital now for two days. How many visitors have you had, apart from me?'

It was a rotten thing to ask, but I wanted to know.

'Just you, Larry. No one else,' and again she smiled.

'So all the old women who pester you for hand-outs haven't been to see you?'

'You're not proving anything, Larry. You don't understand. They are all very poor, and it is a tradition that when you go to a hospital you bring something. They haven't anything to bring, so they stay away.'

I nodded.

'Thanks for explaining it.'

She asked suddenly, 'How's your problem, Larry?'

'Problem?' For a brief moment I didn't know what she meant, then I remembered I was supposed to have a problem, that I was grieving over the loss of Judy, that I had been in a car crash, that I couldn't concentrate on my work and her uncle had advised a change of scene. For the past two days, I hadn't even thought of this problem.

'I think the problem is lost,' I said.

'I thought so.' She regarded me. 'Then you had better go back. This town isn't your neck of the woods.'

I thought of Rhea.

'I'll stick around a little longer. Anything I can bring you tomorrow?'

'You're being an angel, Larry. Thank you ... I'd love something to read.'

I bought a copy of Elia Kazan's *The Arrangement*, and had it sent to her room. I thought this book was about her weight.

FOUR

I drove to Jenny's office, found parking with a tussle, then walked up the six flights of stairs.

Since I had left Jenny, I had returned to the hotel. I had stayed in my dreary little room for around half an hour, during that time I had thought of Rhea Morgan. I had paced up and down while my mind dwelt erotically on her. I wanted her so badly it was like a raging virus in my blood. The thought of stripping off her clothes and taking her made sweat run down my face, but I reminded myself of what she had said: *Man! Don't you want me! When you have me, it'll cost you more than a meal.*

But I wasn't a sucker like Jenny. When I had her, as I was going to have her, it wasn't going to cost me a dime.

But first, I had to know a lot more about her. Jenny would have kept her record and I now wanted to read it. It might give me a lever to turn an attempt to bargain into a sale.

This was my thinking, so I drove to Jenny's office.

I paused outside her office door. Through the thin panels I could hear the clack of a typewriter, and this surprised me. I knocked, turned the handle and walked in.

A thin, elderly woman sat behind the desk. Her face looked as if it had been chopped with a blunt axe out of teak. Squashed in a corner was a teenager doing a peck and hunt routine on the typewriter. They both stared at me as if I had landed from the moon.

'I'm Larry Carr,' I said and gave Hatchet-face my best smile. 'I've been working with Jenny Baxter.'

She was a professional welfare worker—not like Jenny: no

63

sucker. I could imagine the old women would take one look at her and then scuttle.

'Yes, Mr. Carr?' She had a voice a cop would envy.

'I thought I'd look in,' I said, my eyes moving to the filing cabinets that stood behind the teenager who had stopped typing. She was just out of High School, very earnest, completely sexless and a drag. Somewhere in those cabinets, I thought I would find Rhea's background. 'If I can be of help . . .' I let it hang.

'Help?' Hatchet-face stiffened. 'Are you qualified, Mr. Carr?'

'No, but I've . . .' I stopped. I was wasting my breath. I was sure she knew about me.

'Thank you, Mr. Carr.' She stared me over. 'We can manage very well.'

'I just thought I'd look in.' I backed towards the door. 'I'm at the Bendix Hotel. If you want help, just call me.'

'We won't trouble you, Mr. Carr.' Then with a sour grimace, she added, 'Miss Baxter was always calling on amateurs. That's not my method.'

'That I can imagine,' I said and stepped into the passage and closed the door.

I would have liked to have done it legally, but if the old cow was this way, then I would have to do it illegally. I still had the key Jenny had given me to the office.

So I walked down the six flights of stairs and out on to the cement-dusty street. The time was 1700 and I walked to a bar opposite and sat in a corner where I could survey the entrance to the office block. I ordered beer, lit a cigarette and waited.

Time moved on. People came and went. A bar-fly tried to get talking with me, but I brushed him off. After a second beer, taken slowly, I saw Hatchet-face and the teenager emerge and walk together down the street. Hatchet-face held the teenager's arm in a possessive grip as if she expected some man would leap out and rape the girl.

I was in no hurry. I had a third beer, smoked yet another cigarette, then getting to my feet, I walked out on to the street. By now it was 1815. Two giggling girls, in mini skirts, came out of the office block as I entered. In another hour it would be dark. I didn't want to turn on the lights in the office. That could be a giveaway. I walked up the six flights of stairs. The owners of the one-room offices were going home. They brushed by me as I climbed: little men, tall men, fat men, thin men: some with their typists. They didn't notice me. They were too eager to get back to the discomfort of their homes, to eat, to watch television and then go to bed with their dreary wives.

As I reached the sixth floor, a woman with a face like a wrinkled prune came out of an office, slammed the door shut and edged by me as if I were the Boston Strangler. I unlocked Jenny's door, slid into the tiny office, shut the door and turned the key.

It took me some ten minutes to find Rhea Morgan's file. I sat at the desk and read her case history the way I would have read my own case history.

Jenny had done a good job. The report was written in her sprawling handwriting. She must have felt it was too personal for a helper to type.

Rhea Morgan, I learned, was now twenty-eight years of age. At the age of eight, she had come before the law as uncontrollable. She had been sent to a home. At the age of ten she had been caught stealing lipstick and perfume from a self-service store. She had been sent back to the home. At the age of thirteen, she had had sexual relations with one of the executives of the home. They had been caught in the act and a few hours later, before the police arrived, the executive had cut his throat. She had been moved to a stricter home. After a year, she had run away. A year later, she had been picked up while prostituting herself to truck drivers on a freeway to New York. She had come before the law again and had been sent for psychiatric treatment. No success there for she had slipped away and had gone missing for two years. She had then been picked up in Jacksonville with three men who were attempting a bank robbery. There had been a plea for her age and she drew a year. By this time, she would be around seventeen years of age. After serving the sentence, she dropped out of sight, then she reappeared three years later. This time she was involved with two men in a jewel robbery. She was handling the getaway car. The two men, armed with toy pistols, had walked into a cheap jewellery store in Miami. They were amateurs and came apart at the seams when a guard appeared with a ·45 automatic in his fist. Rhea could have driven away, but she stuck and was arrested. With her past record, she drew four years. Out again, she was involved with three men in a gas station hold-up. This time the judge threw the book at her and she went away for another four years, and that was her life up-to-date.

I dropped the report on the desk and lit a cigarette. I now knew her background and I was now curious about her brother. I searched through the files, but came up with nothing. It looked as if Jenny had had no dealings with him, but I was sure he was in Rhea's league.

As the light began to fade, I sat on the desk and thought of Rhea. I thought of the life she had led and I found I was envying her. I thought of my own dull home life, and my mother, kind, who had died when I was fifteen years old, and my father who had slaved in a diamond mine, had made a lot of money, had invested badly and had been defeated when he had died. Rhea had lived a vicious life, but she hadn't been defeated. The moment she had got out of prison, she had followed her destiny of crime. At least she had purpose and drive. The purpose was bad, but she had set her signals and had driven ahead.

Bad?

I crushed out my cigarette and lit another.

I had been taught that stealing was bad, but was it in this modern world in which I lived? Wasn't it rather the survival of the fittest? Wasn't it a brave, private war waged by one individual against the police? Wasn't that better than living the dreary life the people lived who scrounged on Jenny?

Half my mind told me I was wrong, but the other half argued. I knew Rhea had suddenly become the most important person in my life. The fascination was sexual, but also there was this envy that she could have more courage than I had. I wanted suddenly to experience what she had experienced. She had been hunted by the police. This was an experience that I found myself wanting. I thought of how she must have felt when the pressure was on and yet she hadn't panicked and driven away from the jewellery store. I envied her that experience. I felt the urge to find out if I had the guts, under pressure that she had.

It was getting dark now so I returned the report to the filing cabinet, emptied my ash and two cigarette butts into an envelope which I put in my pocket. I didn't want Hatchet-face to know someone had been in the office, then I left.

As I walked down the stairs, I kept thinking of Rhea, with her brother in the sordid bungalow, and I envied them.

Judy?

I continued to walk down the stairs.

Judy was dead, I told myself, but Rhea was alive.

What I should have done was to have checked out of the Bendix Hotel and driven back to Paradise City. I should have talked to Dr. Melish and put myself in his hands. I should have told him I had met a woman with a vicious criminal record and had become sexually obsessed with her. I should have confessed to him that I now had an overpowering urge to do what she had done, trying to explain that when I had her, she and I had to be on equal terms: I as bad as she was, and she as bad as I was. I should have admitted that, because I was male and she was female, I had this thought now hammering in my mind that whatever she could do, I could do better. Maybe it would have helped me. I don't know because I never gave him the chance. I didn't check out of the hotel, nor did I run away to Paradise City.

I sat in a dreary bar and toyed with a stale sandwich and a beer and thought about Rhea. Finally, I got in the Buick and drove out to her place.

She was pulling me with such magnetic force I was powerless to resist.

At the top of the dirt road, I parked the car, turned off the lights and walked the rest of the way. As I approached the bungalow I could hear strident jazz from a transistor, blaring across the debris. Then I came around the slight bend in the lane and saw the lighted windows.

I went as far as the broken-down fence and I stood in the shadow of a tree, looking at the windows the way a man lost in a sun-scorched desert looks at an oasis without knowing it is a mirage.

It was a hot night and the air was close. The windows were open. The time was 2200. I saw a figure move across the light ... the brother. So he was there! I moved cautiously forward, picking my way through the empty cans, the oil drums, stepping carefully to make no noise, but I need not have taken this precaution. With the transistor going at full blast I could have made any noise and still not have been heard.

With my heart thumping, I got close enough to be able to see through the window and yet still not be seen.

Now, I could see the brother clearly. He was stomping around the room in time with the music, an open can in one hand, a spoon in the other. While he stomped, he kept shovelling some gooey looking mess into his mouth. I looked beyond him and found Rhea. She lolled in a beat-up chair, the leather split, the dirty stuffing showing. She had on a red smock and pants that could have been painted on her. I felt my heartbeat quicken at the sight of her long legs and slim thighs. A cigarette dangled from her thin hard lips. She was staring up at the ceiling, her face an expressionless marble mask, while he continued to jerk, weave and stomp to the music as he fed himself.

As I stood there watching, I wondered what was going on in her mind. What a couple! Part of my sane mind said this, but the other half was envious. Then suddenly she leaned forward and snapped off the transistor that stood on a chair by her side. The silence that descended over the bungalow and around me was like a physical blow.

'Cut it out!' she yelled at him. 'Must you always act like a goddamn moron?'

Her brother stood motionless, his shoulders hunched, his hands held forward. His attitude was threatening.

'What the stinking hell do you mean?' he bellowed. 'Turn it on!'

She picked up the transistor, got to her feet and with vicious violence, threw it against the wall. The case broke open and the batteries fell out.

He was across the room and his open hand slapped her across the face, sending her reeling. In four letter words, he yelled at her and then hit her again.

I was already on the move, the forest fire of rage blazing inside me. I charged into the room as he was raising his hand to slap her again. I caught his wrist, swung him around and drove my fist into his face. He went staggering away. I jumped after him and while he was still off balance, and half dazed, I hit him in the groin.

He gave a low moan as he dropped to his knees. I stood over him, laced my fingers together and hit down on his neck with both hands. I didn't give a goddamn if I killed him as I hadn't cared if I had killed Spooky Jinx. He stretched out, unconscious, at my feet.

I turned and looked at Rhea, who was leaning against the wall. Her left cheek showed a bruise. She was still a little dazed from the slaps she had had, but her eyes were on the still body of her brother.

'He's all right,' I said. 'Don't worry about him. Are you all right?' The fire of rage inside me was now dying. 'I just happened by.'

She knelt beside her brother and turned him over. Blood leaked from his nose, but he was breathing. She looked up at me, her green eyes glittering.

'Get out! You're not wanted here!' Her voice was vicious. 'Get out and stay out!'

We stared at each other for a long moment.

'When you're ready,' I said, 'you'll find me at the Bendix Hotel. I'll wait.'

I went out into the hot, dark night, aware my knuckles were aching from the punch I had rammed into his face but not caring.

I drove back to Luceville. I had made a step forward, I told myself. I had shown her I was a better man than her brother. But that wasn't enough. I had to prove to myself that I had more guts than she had.

The telephone in my dreary little hotel bedroom was ringing as I walked in. I hesitated for a brief moment, then I lifted the receiver.

'Larry ... my dear, sweet boy!'

My mind crawled back into the past. No one else could talk like this except Sydney Fremlin.

I dropped on the bed.

'Hi, Sydney.'

He told me he had been trying to reach me. He didn't know *how* many times he had called the hotel, but I was always out. The reproach in his voice made no impact on me.

'How are you, Larry? When are you coming back? I *need* you!'

My mind shifted away from his burbling voice and I thought of Rhea with her bruised face.

'Larry! Are you listening?'

'I'll be back,' I said. 'Give me a little more time. Maybe in a month ... how's that?'

'A month?' His voice shot up. 'But, Larry, I need you here *now*! People keep asking for you. Tell me how you are. Couldn't you come back next week?'

'Isn't Terry doing a job?'

'Terry?' His voice rose a notch. 'Don't mention him to me! He's quite ... unspeakable! Come back, Larry, and I'll throw him out!'

I was bored with him and cut him short.

'I'll be back but not for a month.'

'A month?' Sydney's voice rose to a squeak.

'That's it,' and I hung up.

I went to the bathroom and let cold water run over my aching hand. The telephone started up again. That would be Sydney. I ignored the bell. After a long, desperate try, it stopped ringing.

I stretched out on the bed.

My thoughts made me feel ten feet tall.

I was quite a man, I told myself. Spooky ... seven of his thugs ... now I had taken care of Rhea's brother.

Soon she would come to me. I was sure of this and that was the way I wanted it. For her to come to me and give herself. I was prepared to wait.

But first, I had to get on parity with her.

The usual incentive for most crimes is money, but I had plenty of money so long as Sydney paid me $60,000 a year. Thinking about crime, I realised I was in a unique position. I now wanted to commit a crime so as to experience the same tension, the same danger, the same excitement as Rhea must have experienced, yet I would have no use for whatever I stole. It would be the act of stealing that would give me satisfaction: the end product was of no importance.

I had to break the ice, I told myself. After some thought, I decided the first thing I would steal would be a car. That shouldn't be difficult. I would drive the car around the town, then leave it not too far from where I had stolen it. Once I had done that, I would be a thief ... and this I wanted to be as Rhea was a thief. The chances of getting caught were remote, but the steal would provide a certain amount of tension, and this was what I wanted.

Why think about it? Why not do it?

I looked at my watch. It was eight minutes after midnight.

Still feeling ten feet tall, I put on my jacket, turned off the light and left the room. I didn't use the elevator, but walked silently down the stairs, through the lobby where the night-man was dozing and out into the hot night.

Stealing a car proved more complicated than I had imagined. I walked to the nearest parking lot, but found a guard patrolling, and he looked suspiciously at me, fingering his club as I lingered at the entrance.

'You want something?' he demanded in a cop voice.

'Not you,' I said and moved on.

I tramped down a number of side streets where cars were parked, bumper to bumper. Whenever I paused to see if a car door was unlocked, someone would appear out of the darkness, stare at me, before walking on. I found I was sweating and my heart was thumping. This certainly was tension and I had to

71

admit I didn't like it.

It wasn't until 0100 when my nerves were wilting, that I finally found a car, unlocked and the ignition key in place.

'Here I go,' I thought and wiped my sweating hands on the seat of my jeans. I looked up and down the deserted street, then with my heart pounding, I opened the car door and slid into the driving seat.

With an unsteady hand, I turned on the ignition and pressed down on the gas pedal. There was a faint growling sound which petered out into a whimper. Sweat running down my face, I stared into the car's darkness. I fumbled for the switch to turn on the parkers, found it and the parkers came on: a faint yellow glow which faded into nothing.

I was trying to steal a car with a flat battery!

My nerve cracked. I had had enough tension for one night. I got out of the car, eased the door shut, then started down the street. I had a raging thirst and my thigh muscles were fluttering as if I had run, flat out, a mile.

'So this is tension,' I thought, and yet, what had I done? I had tried to steal a car—something thousands of teenagers did every day of the week—and I hadn't succeeded. Some thief! I thought. How Rhea would have jeered had she known of this gutless performance!

I began to realise that stepping from honesty which had been my background for thirty odd years into dishonesty presented an obstacle that needed more nerve and more courage than I had at this moment.

At the corner, at the end of the street, was an all-night bar. I went in for a beer. There were only three people in the bar: the usual drunk, a fat middle-aged whore and a homosexual: a boy of around eighteen, in a cherry-coloured suit, his hair to his shoulders and around his slim wrist an expensive gold watch. He simpered at me, then seeing his watch, I had a sudden idea. I carried my beer to a distant table, then looked directly at him. He was at my side in an instant.

'Can we be friends?' he asked anxiously. 'I'm sure you're as lonely as I am.'

I stared him over.

'The price?'

'Ten dollars ... I'll give you a wonderful time.'

'Have you a pad?'

'There's a hotel up the street ... they know me.'

I finished the beer and got to my feet.

'So what are we waiting for?'

We went out into the hot darkness and started down the street. He smiled anxiously at me from time to time, keeping close to me as if he was afraid of losing me. He drew away from me as we passed a cop who stared at us and then spat in the gutter.

'It's not far, dear,' the boy said, 'just at the end of the street.'

I looked back. The cop was out of sight and there was no one to be seen. We were passing an alley lined with stinking trash bins. I caught hold of him and shoved him into the alley.

He gave a startled squeak of protest, but it was no more than a squeak. I took pleasure in hitting him because his kind wasn't my kind. My fist thudded against his jaw and I eased him down into the muck, letting his head fall on a pile of mouldy potato peelings. Then bending over him, I took off his gold watch—probably a present from an infatuated client. With a quick look up and down the street, I walked away.

I headed back to my hotel.

Passing another stinking trash bin, I paused to drop the watch into it. I moved some litter to cover the watch and then walked on.

Now, I really felt ten feet tall.

I had broken the ice. I was a thief!

I woke the next morning from a restless sleep and I heard a voice speaking clearly in my mind. The voice was saying, 'You must leave here this morning and go back to Paradise City. You must see Dr. Melish and tell him what is happening to you. You must tell him what you did last night and ask for his help.'

I became fully awake and looked around the room. The voice had been so loud and clear that I thought someone was in

73

the room.

Then I realised I had been dreaming and I dropped back on the pillow.

There was no question of going back. Melish couldn't help me because I didn't want to be helped. I thought of Rhea and my desire for her became so bad, I had to get out of bed and stand under the cold shower until the heat of my body diminished. Then I shaved, put on the sweat shirt and jeans and went down to the restaurant to drink two cups of bad coffee.

There were several elderly salesmen eating breakfast while they consulted their notebooks. None of them paid any attention to me. I lit a cigarette and thought about last night.

What a gutless performance!

How Rhea would have sneered had she known!

How I had fumbled the operation of stealing a car! Then this stupid little pansy. Anyone could have done that! What risk had I taken? I had stolen his watch which was probably his dearest possession. That was nothing to be proud of. I remembered Spooky Jinx had called me Cheapie. On my record of last night that was exactly what I was: Cheapie.

But tonight, I told myself, would be different. Tonight, I was determined to move into the big league, but this needed planning. I sat there, smoking and thinking, and finally I came up with a plan of operation.

Leaving the hotel, I got into the Buick and drove out of town. Some hundred miles north on the freeway was a little town called Jason's Halt. It was an orange-growing town: clean, prosperous and small. Its main street was crowded with trucks and orange brokers doing deals. I found parking space, then walked along the hot sidewalk until I found a self-service store. I shoved my way through the crowd, busy getting in the week-end groceries: a surging mass of people, and to them, I was the invisible man.

I found my way to the snack bar, ate a steak sandwich and drank a beer, then took the escalator to the toy department. There, I asked the girl for a toy revolver, mentioning a non-existent nephew. She showed me an assortment of revolvers, automatics and even a Colonel Cody Colt. I chose a Beretta, made famous by 007. It was an exact replica and looked menacing when I held it in my hand. I then went down to a lower floor and bought a sling bag with TWA stamped on its sides. From there I went to the men's shop and after a search, I bought a dark red jacket with black patch pockets: a jacket that would be remembered. From there, I went into the gimmick department and bought a Beatle wig and a pair of silvered sun-glasses through which you could see, but rendered your face anonymous.

All these items I put in the sling bag.

I got back to Luceville around 1615.

As I was driving to the hotel I passed the city hospital and I remembered I hadn't seen Jenny and she would be wondering about me. A car pulled out from a parking bay, so I drove into the space, acting on impulse. I sat for some minutes trying to make up my mind if I wanted to see Jenny again. I was inclined not to see her, but the other part of my mind pulled. I got out of the car and walked over to the bookstall and bought a copy of Forsyth's *Day of the Jackal* and Graham Greene's great classic, *The Power and the Glory*.

'I was wondering about you,' Jenny said after thanking me for the books. 'I wish you would go home.'

'Don't fuss.' I smiled at her, thinking how different she was to Rhea. 'I'm not yet ready for the lush and plush life of Paradise City.'

'But what are you doing?'

I shrugged.

'I get around. This town fascinates me.'

'You have hurt your hand.'

My knuckles were still raw from hitting Rhea's brother.

'I had trouble with my car ... the spanner slipped. How are you, Jenny?'

'Mending. The ankle takes time.'

I told her about Hatchet-face and the teenager.

'She doesn't want me.'

'Miss Mathis is very professional.' Jenny shook her head. 'Do you mind?'

'I can't say I do.' A pause, then I asked her what I wanted

to know. 'Tell me something, Jenny ... Rhea Morgan's brother ... he seemed a tough character. What does he do for a living or don't you know?'

'Fel?'

'Is that his name ... Fel Morgan?'

'Feldon ... his grandfather was Feldon Morgan. He was named after him. His grandfather was shot while robbing a bank.'

'He was? Do you know how Fel makes a living?'

'Something to do with junk cars ... selling scrap ... that sort of thing. Why are you interested?'

'That bungalow ... what a place! I didn't think anyone making any kind of a living could live there.'

'Oh yes. Some people just don't care where or how they live.' She made a grimace. 'I worry about Rhea. She could so easily get into trouble again. Her brother's no help. She has this obsession about getting rich. She just won't accept the fact that if you want money you must work for it ... she says she won't wait that long. I've talked to her so often, but I can't get through. I'm beginning to think she's a hopeless case. I hate saying this about anyone, but Rhea could be a hopeless case. I feel she will be in trouble again soon and then she will go back to prison for years.'

'Well, it's her funeral,' I said. 'But it does tell me what a tough job you have.'

She lifted her hand and dropped it on the sheet.

'I'm not complaining. It's my job.' A pause, then she went on, 'People have to live their own lives. Every so often, I feel I do influence them and that is rewarding.' She smiled at me. 'Can't I influence you, Larry, just a little? Won't you go home and forget this town ... just to please me?'

Thoughts flashed through my mind. Jenny was a Do-gooder: a woman walking up an escalator going the other way. I had other things on my mind. This was the opportunity to con her. She would be laid up for another two weeks and couldn't check on me.

I made out I was hesitating, then I nodded as if I had made up my mind.

'All right, Jenny, you have influenced me,' I said. I'll go.
You're right: I am wasting my time here. I hate leaving you.
You've been a good friend to me, but you're right. I'll go first
thing tomorrow.'

Maybe I overdid it. Maybe she was smarter than I gave her
credit for. She looked sadly at me.

'I've learned people do have to live their own lives. Very
few people will take advice. I try, but they don't listen, so
there isn't much I can do about it, is there?'

I suddenly wanted to tell her what was happening to me. I
knew I would never tell Dr. Melish, but there was something
about her as she lay in the bed, looking searchingly at me that
gave me the urge to confide in her.

Then Rhea came into my mind and the moment to confess
had gone.

I touched her fingers, forced a smile, said a few banal things
about keeping in touch and then walked out of the hospital, my
mind switched to what I had to do this night.

Back in my hotel bedroom, I unpacked the items I had
bought. I put on the jacket, then the wig, then the silver
glasses. With the Beretta toy gun in my hand, I went into the
shower room where there was a full-length mirror.

I looked at myself.

I certainly looked a freak, and I was sure no one could
possibly recognise me. I drew my lips off my teeth in a snarl
and I looked scarey. I lifted the gun and pointed it at my
reflection and I snarled: 'This is a goddamn hold-up!'

If this threatening image in the mirror had walked into my
office in Paradise City I would have handed over all the diamonds in the safe without hesitation.

Satisfied, I took off the wig, the glasses and the jacket and
packed them carefully, with the gun, in the sling bag. I felt
sure that by taking the trouble of buying them in Jason's Halt
there would be no chance of the police, after the raid, tracing
them to me.

I was pleased with myself.

Now I had to wait until midnight and then I would be in
the big league.

I lay on the bed and rehearsed the operation. I went through the dialogue I would use. Having satisfied myself I was word perfect, I dropped off to sleep. I was pleased I could sleep. This proved to me that there was nothing wrong with my nerves.

Around 2100, I woke and went across the street to a snack bar and ate greasy meatballs and spaghetti. I took my time. Leaving the snack bar, I returned to the hotel, collected the sling bag and then walked to my car which I had parked at the end of the street.

I drove out of town and along the freeway. Five miles out of Luceville was a Caltex service station. I had never stopped there, but I had often passed it. It was always doing a brisk trade, and I knew it remained open all night.

As I drove by it, I slowed the Buick. There was a fat, powerfully built man in white uniform shooting gas into a car. I couldn't see anyone else around. I felt satisfied this man was on night shift and would be on his own.

I U-turned when I could and drove back to Luceville. I spent the next two hours in an all-night movie house, watching an old Western. It was good enough to hold my attention.

When the lights came up, I walked with the rest of the crowd into the hot cement-dusty street and got in my car.

For some moments, I sat still, before starting the motor.

Here I go, I thought and was a little dismayed that my heart was thumping and my hands wet with sweat.

There was a lay-by some three hundred yards from the service station. I pulled into it, killed the motor and the lights. I looked ahead at the bright flashing sign that spelt out: C A L-T E X. Getting out of the car and keeping in the shadows, I put on the jacket, the wig and the glasses. My hands were so unsteady, when I took the toy gun out of the sling bag I dropped it. I spent some feverish moments groping in the grass before I found it.

My heart was hammering. For a moment I hesitated whether to go back to the hotel or to go ahead.

Then Rhea with her red hair and her cynical, sexy green eyes came into my mind and my nerve stiffened.

I walked fast along the grass verge of the highway towards the lights of the service station.

Only an occasional car whizzed by me.

As I neared the service station I slowed my pace.

Keeping in the shadows, I moved slowly forward. I could now see the small, well-lighted office. The fat attendant was watching a late-night TV show, a cigarette dangling from his lips.

Tension was making my heart beat so violently I had trouble with my breathing. I stood still for some minutes, watching him. The highway was deserted. If I was going to do it, I had to do it now.

I heard myself muttering: 'Are you crazy? You could land in jail!' But I moved forward, gripping the butt of the toy gun so hard my fingers began to ache.

The attendant looked up as I pushed open the glass door. At the sight of me, he stiffened, then seeing the gun, he froze.

'This is a hold up,' I said, but there was no snarl in my voice. I was as scared as he was.

We stared at each other. He was a man around fifty years of age: a fat, fatherly type, his hair shot with grey and he had steady brown eyes and the firm mouth of a provider.

He recovered from his fright. His eyes examined the gun in my hand, then he relaxed.

'No money here, son,' he said quietly. 'You're out of luck.'

'Give me the money or this heater goes off.' The quaver in my voice sickened me. I knew I was as menacing as a mouse.

'We have a system here, son,' he said, as if talking to a child. 'A night safe. Every buck I get gets fed into that steel box over there and only the boss can open it.'

I stared at him, sweat running down my face.

'I gave my son one of those guns for Christmas,' he went on. 'He's crazy about James Bond.' His eyes shifted to the lighted TV screen. 'Suppose you shove off? Maybe I'm old-fashioned, but I go for Bob Hope.' He gave a relaxed laugh as Hope said: *Even my flab is flabby.*

Defeated, I went away into the darkness, to my car and back to the hotel.

FIVE

Back in my hotel bedroom, I lay in the dark and in despair.
Cheapie!
Spooky's taunt rang in my ears.
Yes ... Cheapie!
My head ached and I was shivering with frustration and
shame. I was gutless! There must be something wrong with
my mechanism! It was only when I was goaded into losing my
temper that I seemed to be able to act, but in cold blood, I was
as menacing as a mouse!

I knew for certain that my gutless attempt to compete with
Rhea's record was now stillborn. I knew I hadn't the guts to
make a second attempt, sure that it would lead to my arrest. I
was a hopeless, useless, fumbling amateur! I had been lucky
with the fat attendant. He had known as soon as he saw the
gun that it was a toy, and he had dismissed me with the contempt I deserved.

My mind switched to Rhea. My body ached for her. I was
past telling myself I was crazy, that the evil and the viciousness in her could destroy me. There was her siren's song
hammering in my mind, and it was irresistible.

I remembered what she had said: *When you have me it'll
cost you more than a meal.* I remembered how she had looked,
standing there, her green eyes full of sexual promises, her body
slightly arched towards me, her sensual smile.

And now I didn't give a damn what it would cost me! Gone
was my arrogant confidence that I would have her for nothing.
I had to have her! I had to have her even on her own terms!
What would she want? Jenny had written in her report that

this woman had been a prostitute. Suppose I offered her two hundred dollars? That was a hell of a price to pay a whore. She wouldn't refuse two hundred dollars! Maybe once I had taken her, I would get her out of my system.

I began to relax, although my head still ached. Impatiently, I got out of bed, threw eight Aspro tablets into my mouth and washed them down. I got back to bed and waited for the pills to work. Money bought anything, I told myself, providing you had enough money. I would buy her! *She has this obsession about getting rich,* Jenny had said, Rhea, I told myself, would jump at two hundred dollars. I didn't care now that I was buying her. My overpowering lust that was tormenting me demanded the sight of her naked, on a bed. Then once I had taken her, once this lust was satisfied, I would return to Paradise City and forget her.

Still thinking, I finally fell asleep.

The following morning, feeling much more confident, I went to the local bank and cashed five one-hundred-dollar Traveller's cheques. Just to be on the safe side, I told myself. I would offer her two hundred and go to five if I had to, but I was sure she would grab the two hundred.

I returned to where I had parked the Buick, started the motor, then as I was about to engage gear, I remembered her brother. Would he be there? Would he be hanging around that sordid little bungalow? My fingers tightened on the driving wheel. I couldn't make my offer if he were in the bungalow.

This was a problem and a wave of sick frustration ran through me. I turned off the ignition, got out of the car and started down the street. It was too early. The City Hall clock was striking ten o'clock. I had to contain my impatience. I would have to wait until at least midday and even then, I couldn't be sure the brother would be away at work. I walked aimlessly, not seeing anyone, Rhea burning a hole in my mind. I wandered around like that until the City Hall clock struck eleven. By then I was fit to climb a tree. I went into a bar and called for a double Scotch on the rocks.

The drink steadied me a little. I lit a cigarette and just as I was going to call for another drink, I saw Fel Morgan across

81

the street, getting out of a dusty 1960 Buick.

I hurriedly paid for my drink and went quickly to the bar entrance. Fel was already walking away, his hands in his jeans pockets: a tight, dirty white Tee shirt outlining his powerful muscles.

I went after him, following him to a scrap metal yard. I paused to watch him enter and wave to a fat man in overalls who was struggling with a vast lump of rusty metal.

With my heart hammering and my breath coming in gasps, I spun round and raced back along the street to where I had parked my car. I sent it shooting towards Highway 3.

Twenty minutes later I was bumping up the dirt road that led to the Morgan's bungalow.

I kept muttering to myself: 'Please God, let her be in!'

As I pulled up outside the bungalow, I saw the front door was standing open. I switched off the motor and sat still, my hands gripping the steering wheel, listening to the thump of my heart while I stared at the open door. I sat there for a minute or so, then I got out of the car and, in a sexual fever, walked slowly over the rough grass, picking my way through the litter.

As I reached the open front door, Rhea appeared in the doorway that led to the sitting-room.

We stood looking at each other.

She had smartened herself up since last I had seen her. She had on a skimpy cotton dress that reached to just above her knees. Her legs and feet were bare. Around her neck was a cheap blue necklace. Her face was as cold and as expressionless as ever and her green eyes as cynical.

'Hello,' she said in her husky voice that sent shivers through me. 'What do you want?'

Trying to keep my voice steady, I said, 'You know what I want.'

She studied me and then stepped back.

'Better come in and talk about it.'

I followed her into the sordid little room. A chipped coffee pot and two used cups stood on the table. A tin ashtray, spilling over with butts, made a centre-piece.

82

I watched her walk over to the ruined armchair and sink into it. Her dress rode up to her thighs and as she crossed her legs I caught a glimpse of blue pantees.

'I thought the idea was you were going to wait until I came to you.' She reached for a pack of cigarettes lying on the table.

'How much?' I said hoarsely. 'Don't light that! How much and let's get on with it!'

She struck a match and lit the cigarette and she smiled jeeringly.

'Man! How you want it,' she said.

With a shaking hand I took two one-hundred-dollar bills from my hip pocket and tossed them into her lap.

'Let's get on with it!'

She picked up the bills and regarded them, her face expressionless, then she looked up at me. I was hoping to see a flash of greed, even pleasure, but this cold mask of a face chilled me.

'What's this supposed to be for? Two hundred bucks? You want your head examined.'

That was the most truthful thing I was ever to hear from her, but I didn't give a damn. I wanted her with an urgency that was close to madness and I was going to have her.

I pulled out the remaining three one-hundred-dollar bills and threw them at her. Although I lusted for her, I have never hated anyone as I now hated her.

'That's more than you're worth, but take it!' I said violently. 'Now, let's get on with it!'

Slowly and deliberately she folded the five bills neatly and put them on the table. She leaned back in the chair, letting smoke drift down her thin nostrils while she regarded me.

'There was a time when I got laid for a dollar,' she said. 'There was a time when I got laid for twenty dollars. There was even a time when I got laid for a hundred dollars. When you spend years in a cell, you have time to think. I know what men want. I know what you want and I know I have it and I want money: not a hundred dollars nor five hundred dollars nor five thousand dollars: I want real money! There are old, fat, stupid creeps in this country worth millions. I think in millions. I'm going to find one of these old, fat stupid creeps and I'm going to sell him my body for real money. It'll take time, but I'll get him.' She flicked a contemptuous finger at the money on the table. 'Take it away, Cheapie. My legs stay crossed until I find a creep with the money I want.'

I stood there, staring at her.

'Can't you use five hundred dollars?'

'Not your five hundred dollars.'

I wanted her so badly I lost what was left of my pride.

'Why not? Five hundred dollars for half an hour. Come on ... take the money and let's get on with it.'

'You heard what I said, Mr. Larry Diamonds Carr.'

I stiffened and stared at her.

'What are you saying?'

'I know who you are. Fel found out. He got your car number and checked Paradise City. You're a well-known character, aren't you, Mr. Larry Diamonds Carr?'

A red light lit up through my madness, warning me to get away from this woman and stay away, but I was too far gone, and after a moment the red light faded to nothing.

'What does it matter who I am?' I said. 'I'm like any other man! Take the money and strip off!'

'If you don't take it, baby, I will,' Fel said from behind me.

I whirled around to find him leaning up against the door frame, watching me, an evil little grin lighting up his face.

The sight of him brought alive a flicker of that insane rage I had experienced before, and he saw it in my eyes.

'Take is easy, buster,' he said. 'I'm on your side. This bitch is only playing hard to get. You want me to fix her for you?'

Rhea got swiftly to her feet and snatched up the money from the table which she crumpled in her fist.

'You come near me, you creep,' she snarled at her brother, 'and I'll hook your goddam eyes out!'

He laughed.

'And she would too,' he said to me. 'Suppose we all cool off and chat it up? We've been talking about you. We could do a trade. How about swopping some of those diamonds you deal in for some pussy?'

I stared at her.

'How about it, buster?' he went on. 'She'll play. It was her idea when I told her who you were. You won't get it without diamonds. Let's chat it up.'

'Give me back my money,' I said to her.

She smiled jeeringly as she shook her head.

'I've changed my mind. I can use five hundred bucks even if it's yours. And don't try to get it from me. Fel and me can take care of you. Think over what Fel's said. If you want it bad enough, diamonds will buy it. Not one diamond, but a lot of diamonds. Think about it. Now ... get out!'

I looked at Fel and saw he was holding a short iron bar in his hand.

'Don't try it, buster,' he said. 'You'll only get a cracked nut. I wasn't ready for you the first time, but I am now. Think about it. Now, scram!'

He edged back to give me room to pass him.

I hated him.

I hated her too, but my blood still lusted for her.

I went out into the hot smog, across the rough grass and debris and returned to the Buick.

I don't remember driving back to the hotel. I became aware that I was lying on the bed with the mid-morning haze lighting up the cement dust on the window facing me.

A black depression filled my mind. Even Rhea had called me Cheapie! God! How I hated her! I felt a sudden urge to kill myself. I lay on the bed, asking myself 'Why not?' Suddenly this seemed to me to be the solution. Why go on? Why let this woman torment me any longer?

But how do I kill myself? I wondered

A razor? I used an electric shaver.

Aspirins? I had only six left.

Jump out of the window?

I could kill someone in the crowded street.

I looked feverishly around the room. There was nothing that would support my weight on which to hang myself.

The car?

Yes! I'd take the car and at high-speed crash it into a tree. Yes! I would do that!

I struggled off the bed, fumbling in my pockets for the car keys. I couldn't find them. Where had I put them? I looked wildly around the room and saw them lying on the dusty chest-of-drawers. As I moved towards them, the telephone bell rang.

For a long moment I hesitated, then I snatched up the receiver.

'Larry . . . my dear boy!'

My black cloud of depression and madness lifted at the sound of Sydney Fremlin's voice. I found I was shaking and sweating. I dropped on to the bed.

'Hi, Sydney.' My voice was a croak.

'Larry, you *must* come back!' I could tell by his voice that he was in the middle of a major crisis. The pitch of his voice told me he was like a bee captured in a bottle and buzzing like crazy.

'What is it?' I said, wiping the sweat off my face with the back of my hand.

'Larry, precious, I simply can't talk over an open line! Some dreadful person may be listening in! You just *have* to come back! Mrs. P. wants to sell you-know-what! I can't possibly handle this—only clever you can do it! You *do* know what I'm trying to say, don't you, Larry? This is absolutely, terribly top secret! Do tell me you understand?'

Mrs. P.

I drew in a long slow breath as my mind went back five years when I had brought off my biggest diamond sale for Luce & Fremlin. Mrs. Henry Jason Plessington, the wife of one of the richest estate men in Florida—and they don't come richer—had wanted a diamond necklace. She had been a client of Luce & Fremlin for years. Until I had arrived as their diamond expert, Sydney had sold her this and that, but nothing really big. But when I arrived on the scene, had met her, had learned how rich her husband was, I saw the possibility of unloading something really big on her. Sydney fluttered and buzzed, saying I was far too ambitious when I explained the idea I had, but I turned on the charm and talked to this middle-aged woman, stressing that nothing but the best was for her. She reacted to this sales talk like a plant reacts to a dose of fertiliser. Having got her so far, I talked to her about diamonds. I said it was my ambition to create a diamond necklace that would be the end of all diamond necklaces. I explained how I would search for matching stones. It would give me pleasure to know that the end product would be hers. She lapped this up the way a cat laps cream.

'But how do I know I will like it?' she asked. 'Your taste might not be my taste.'

I had expected her to say just this, and I was ready for the answer. I said, apart from showing her a design on paper, I would get a Chinese diamond cutter I knew in Hong Kong to make a mock-up of the necklace in glass. She could then judge for herself. The cost of the mock-up would be around $5,000. Naturally, if she decided to have the mock-up turned into the real thing the $5,000 would come off the bill.

She had said for me to go ahead.

I got Sydney to design the necklace on paper. He had a flair for this kind of thing, and he produced a real beauty.

'But, Larry, in diamonds this will cost the earth!' he exclaimed as we studied his design. 'She'll never stand for it! It'll cost a million!'

'It'll cost more than that,' I said, 'but leave it to me. I'll talk her into talking her husband into it. He's stinking rich.'

Mrs. P. approved the design which was a step forward. I was hoping she would tell me to go ahead and make the necklace in diamonds, but she had still to work on her husband and she liked the idea of seeing the design in glass.

It took two months for my man in Hong Kong to produce the glass necklace and what a job he made of it! Only a top expert would know these stones weren't diamonds. It was so good I had an uneasy feeling that Mrs. P. might settle for the mock-up and swank to her friends that it was the real thing.

I went to Plessington's enormous villa, overlooking the sea, with a Rolls Corniche and a Bentley T standing on the tarmac, I laid the glass necklace on a pad of black velvet and watched her face. She went practically into a swoon. Then I draped the necklace around her fat neck and led her to a full-length mirror.

Then I turned on the sales talk.

'These, of course, as you can see, Mrs. Plessington,' I said, 'are made of glass. Also as you can see there is no life in them (which wasn't true), but I want you to imagine each one of these glass beads as living fire . . . the fire of diamonds.'

She stood there, entranced, looking at herself: a stout, middle-aged woman with a flabby bosom, her neck beginning to wrinkle.

'Even Elizabeth Taylor would want a necklace like this is going to be.'

Then I unclasped the necklace before she got the wrong idea and settled for glass rather than diamonds.

'But what is it going to cost?'

This, of course, was the sixty-four-thousand-dollar question. I explained that to create a necklace like this with diamonds, I would have to search the world for matching stones. Having found them, they would have to be cut by experts, then they would have to be set in platinum which would also have to be done by experts. All this would cost money. I lifted my hands and gave her my charming smile. I knew, as she knew, it wouldn't be her money that would pay for this necklace. She would have to put the bite on her husband. I pointed out that diamonds lived for ever. They never lost their value. Her husband's money would be invested safely. I let her absorb all this, then told her, making my voice completely casual, that the necklace would cost in the region of one million and a half dollars.

She didn't even flinch. Why should she? It would be her husband who would do the flinching. She sat there, a fat heap in a Normal Hartnell creation, a far-away look in her eyes. I could imagine she was thinking how her friends would envy her, what a status symbol this necklace would be and even, perhaps, Liz Taylor, would envy her.

So eventually, Mrs. P got her diamond necklace, the biggest sale Luce & Fremlin had ever made and due to me. The final cost of the necklace was one million, eight hundred thousand dollars.

Mrs. P. and the necklace got a big press coverage. There were photographs of her in the papers wearing the necklace with her husband hovering in the background, looking as if he had bitten into a quince. She showed off the necklace at the Casino, the opera, the Country Club and had a ball. Then a month later one of her closest friends who owned a diamond necklace that I wouldn't have offered to any of my clients, got knocked over the head and the necklace snatched. The woman never recovered from the attack and had to be taken care of by a nurse.

This attack scared the pants off Mr. P. who only then realised that her one-million, eight-hundred-thousand-dollar string of diamonds could be a source of lethal danger. She promptly put the necklace in a safe deposit box at her bank and refused to wear it.

All this took place five years ago, and now, according to Sydney, she wanted to sell the necklace.

I knew, as Sydney knew, that during the past three years, Mrs. P. had become a compulsive gambler. Every night she was to be found at the Casino, plunging. Her husband let her gamble because, apart from selling large slices of Florida and putting up sky-scrapers wherever there was a space for them, he was a ram. While his wife was spending most of the night gambling he was in the hay with any girl who caught his eye. But Plessington looked after his money, and every so often he would check up on his wife's gambling debts and crack down on her. Mrs. P. never won. Knowing this background, it wasn't hard to see that she must now be up to her eyes in secret debt and had decided to sell the necklace before her husband found out what she owed.

'Larry?' Sydney's voice crackled over the line. 'Are you listening?'

I didn't give a damn about Mrs. P., the necklace nor come to that, Sydney. Rhea was still burning a hole in my mind.

'I'm listening,' I said.

'For pity's sake, concentrate, Larry,' Sydney said urgently.

'Please . . . for my sake! You *must* come back! I can't imagine what you are doing in that dreadful town! *Do* say you will come back and help me!'

Again the nudge of destiny. A few minutes ago I was thinking of suicide. If Sydney had wanted me to do anything else except try to resell the Plessington necklace I would have hung up on him. But this necklace, up to now, had been my greatest achievement. I had gained my reputation as one of the top diamond men by creating it.

My depression suddenly went away. My mind worked swiftly. Maybe another change of scene would get Rhea out of my blood, but I wanted a back door through which to escape if the need arose.

'I'm still not right, Sydney,' I said. 'I get headaches and concentration isn't easy. If I come back and sell you-know-what, will you give me more time off if I need it?'

'Of course, dear boy! I'll do more than that. I'll give you one per cent on the take and you can have six months off if you want it. I can't be fairer than that, can I?'

'What does she want for it?'

He buzzed like a bee trapped in a bottle again before saying, 'I haven't discussed it with her. She's panting for money. I said I would consult you and you would talk to her.'

Again I hesitated, thinking of Rhea, then I made up my mind.

'All right. I'll leave right away. I should be with you the day after tomorrow.'

'Don't come by car. Come by air taxi. I'll pick up the tab,' Sydney said. 'You don't know what a relief this is to me! Let's have a quiet dinner together. We'll meet around nine o'clock at La Palma . . . what do you say?'

La Palma was one of the most expensive and exclusive restaurants in Paradise City. Sydney was certainly anxious to please.

'It's a date,' I said and hung up.

During the two-hour flight back to Paradise City, while I was sitting in the little cabin, a thought like a black snake wriggling into a room slid into my mind.

There are old, fat, stupid creeps in this country worth millions.

Rhea had said that.

Why should I wait to become old, fat and stupid?

Why shouldn't I become suddenly immensely rich?

I thought of Mrs. P.'s necklace. One million eight hundred thousand dollars! In my position as a top diamond man, knowing the big diamond dealers throughout the world, I was sure I would have no trouble in selling the stones, always providing I was careful. These dealers would jump at anything I had to offer. I had often sold diamonds to them for Sydney, who always wanted to be paid in cash. The dealers never questioned this, as when Sydney bought from them he also paid cash, and—what was important—they accepted my receipt.

By breaking up the necklace, selling the stones to various dealers would present no problem. In my position at Luce & Fremlin I would have no need to worry, as Sydney no longer kept contact with these dealers. He left them to me to handle. They would pay me cash, thinking the money was going to Sydney and I would put the money in a Swiss bank. Disposing of the necklace was the least of my headaches, but stealing it so that no one suspected me was something else.

This seemed to me to be a challenge. Maybe I was useless as a hold-up man and gutless when it came to stealing a car, but this operation of stealing the necklace, although a problem, was, at least, in my neck of the woods.

I spent the next hour as the little plane droned on to Paradise City thinking of ways and means.

I found Sydney sitting in a discreet alcove, toying with a double martini. The maître d' of La Palma restaurant conducted me to him as if I were a member of a Royal family.

As usual, the restaurant was crowded and I had to pause at several tables where my clients greeted me and asked after my health, but finally I reached the alcove and Sydney gripped my hand.

'Larry, dear boy, you just don't know how I appreciate this!' he gushed and there were tears in his eyes. 'You don't look well ... you look peaky. How are you? Was the flight a strain? I hate myself for bringing you back here, but you do understand, don't you?'

'I'm all right,' I said. 'Don't fuss, Sydney. The flight was fine.'

But he wouldn't leave it alone. First, he ordered a double dry martini for me, and when the maître d' had gone he asked questions about my health, what I had been doing with myself and finally if I had missed him.

I was used to his buzzing and finally cut him short.

'Look, Sydney, let's get down to business. I'm a little tired, and after dinner I want to go to bed, so don't let's waste time about my health.'

The dry martini arrived and Sydney then ordered caviar, a lobster soufflé and champagne.

'Will that be all right, Larry?' he asked. 'It's light and nourishing and you will sleep well on it.'

I said it would be fine.

'So she wants to sell the necklace?' I said when the maître d' had gone away, snapping his fingers at two waiters to ensure we got top service.

'She came in yesterday ... quivering like a jelly,' Sydney said. 'I've known the poor thing for years, and she regards me as one of her closest friends. She confessed to me she just had to have a large sum of money and Henry mustn't know. I thought at first she was going to put the bite on me, and my brain was simply spinning to think of an excuse, but she came right out with it. She had to sell the necklace, and Henry must—repeat—must not know. What would I give her for it?'

'Gambling again?'

'She didn't say, but of course ... she must be in the hole for thousands. Of course, as soon as I knew what was in the wind, I enveloped myself in a smoke screen. I said you would have to deal with the sale. You were my diamond man and you could be relied on to be as silent as the tomb. I said you were out of town, but as soon as you came back I would ask you to call on her. The poor thing nearly peed herself. She said she couldn't

wait. When would you be back? It was terribly,
urgent. I said I would try to get you back tonight, and
it at that. Well, you're back. Will you see her tomorrow
ing, Larry? You have no idea the state she's in. She's
silly stupid and I hate to see her suffer. You will see her,
you?'

'That's why I'm here.'

The caviar arrived, and while we were buttering the to
went on, 'You have no idea how much she wants?'

'I kept my little mouth shut about that. I didn't wan
spoil your ploy. I didn't ask questions. It's all yours, Larry.'

I spread the caviar on the toast.

'This could be tricky, Sydney,' I said. 'You realise,
course, the necklace will have to be broken up? We couldn
hope to sell it as it is. Publicity would start up again and i
Plessington saw a photo of some other woman wearing the
necklace, Mrs. P. would be shot down. I've been thinking
about this in the plane. We could do a hell of a deal for ourselves: we might even sell those diamonds for two million
dollars, but it would have to be worked carefully.'

Sydney's eyes bulged.

'Two million?'

'The way I see it is this: I go talk to Mrs. P. I explain that
if she is willing for us to sell the necklace as it stands, we will
pay her a million, eight hundred thousand—what she paid for
it. From what you tell me—and I'll underline that the resale
of the necklace will receive the same press treatment as when
she bought it—once she knows this, she will be too scared to
let us sell it as it is. Over that hurdle, I will explain to her the
necklace will lose a lot of its value once it is broken up. I will
tell her it will mean trying to sell the stones separately, and we
couldn't offer her more than nine hundred thousand ... half
the original price. If she agrees to this—and she might—then
you pay her nine hundred thousand, and we have the necklace.'
I held up my hand as he was about to interrupt. 'Let me finish.
You must design a diamond collar that will take all Mrs. P.'s
diamonds. I'll get Chan to make up the collar and I'll look
around for someone either in South America or India or the

iiddle-East and unload the collar on whoever it is for two
illion. You will then be making one million one hundred
housand dollars profit which seems to me to be a pretty nice
eal.'

He sat back, his caviar forgotten. For a long moment he
tared at me. 'But we can't do that!' He looked shocked. 'We
can't make a profit like that out of that poor, poor thing.'

'This is business, Sydney,' I said, spreading more caviar.
'You ask Tom if we can't do it.'

He threw up his hands.

'Tom has the soul of a computer and a heart of a cash
register.'

'That's why you are eating caviar.'

He munched for a few moments while he brooded.

'You really think you can sell this necklace for two million?'

'Why not?' I was sure I couldn't, but this was the bait I had
decided to dangle under Sydney's nose. 'Even the Burtons
might buy it for that, but it would be up to you to design a
collar that would make every other diamond collar yet de-
signed second class.'

His eyes brightened. This was the kind of challenge Sydney
loved.

'I'm sure I could do that! What a wonderful idea, Larry!
What a clever puss you are!'

I saw I had him sold and I began to relax. We paused to
drink some champagne, then I edged on to the really thin
ice.

'This will take time, Sydney. I'll have to fly to Hong Kong.
Chan will take at least a month to make the collar. It'll take at
least three or even five months to sell the collar. In the
meantime what happens to Mrs. P.?'

He gaped at me. This hadn't occurred to him.

'I knew it was too good to be true! She can't wait! I don't
believe she can wait a week!'

The waiter came and took away the plates. We both sat
silent until the lobster soufflé was served and the waiter had
withdrawn.

I then dropped my little bomb: not knowing if it would go

off or not.

'As I see it, Sydney, if we're going to do this deal, you'll have to lend her the money until the collar is sold.'

His eyes opened wide.

'Nine hundred thousand?' His voice went up into a squeak.

'You lend it to her at six per cent and finally you sell the necklace for two million,' I said. 'Ask Tom if this isn't an outstanding deal.'

'But I can't afford to lend her all that money!'

'I'm not saying you lend her the money. The firm lends it to her.'

'Tom would never, never lend anyone anything even if it was Nixon!'

'Okay, so you lend the money. Your bank will give you an overdraft. What have you to lose? You will get the necklace. Even if I can't get two million for it—and I think I can—I'll get what she paid for it. Even at that you will be doubling your money. Come on, Sydney . . . this is a chance in a lifetime!'

He forked some of the soufflé into his mouth while he thought, and I saw a sudden greedy look come into his eyes.

'Tom needn't know about this, need he?' he said. 'I mean suppose I put up the money—my own personal money—then when you sell the necklace what you get would be my personal money . . . wouldn't it?'

'That's right . . . less one per cent commission for me.'

He looked at me a little narrowly. I saw he hadn't thought of paying me a commission.

'Yes . . . one per cent to you,' and by his expression I saw he was trying to do sums in his head.

'You will give me eighteen thousand dollars and you will deduct Mrs. P.'s nine hundred thousand and you will add Mrs. P.'s six per cent on your loan and you will net yourself roughly eight hundred and eighty thousand which seems to me to be a nice profit.'

He thought some more, then, finally, he said, 'I've got even a better idea, Larry, dear boy. Suppose you try to persuade Mrs. P. to sell the necklace outright for seven hundred and fifty thousand? After all it isn't her money. I could sell stock to cover this amount, and then the necklace would be mine and I wouldn't have to worry about Tom, would I? If I did that and you sold the diamonds for two millions, I could make a million and a quarter ... that's pretty handsome, isn't it?'

'I thought you didn't want to make a profit out of the poor, poor thing,' I said, trying to look shocked.

He shifted uneasily.

'After all it was you who said this is business.' He paused to peer at me. 'Do you think you could persuade her to sell at that price?'

'No harm in trying.' I finished the last of the soufflé.

'See what you can do tomorrow, Larry. I'm sure you can pull it off.' Sydney snapped his fingers at a waiter and ordered coffee. 'I tell you what I'll do ... you get the necklace for seven hundred and fifty thousand and I'll give you two per cent on the deal. I can't be fairer than that, can I?'

'And my air ticket to Hong Kong and all expenses,' I said knowing there would be no Hong Kong.

'Naturally, dear boy.'

'Does Terry know about Mrs. P.?'

'Don't mention that unspeakable boy! I really must get rid of him!' Sydney flushed with annoyance. 'He really is becoming quite, quite impossible!'

'Never mind that ... does he know?'

'Of course not!'

'Are you sure? Mrs. P. came to see you. Didn't he want to know what she wanted?'

'We are not even speaking to each other!'

'He couldn't have listened?' I was nervous of Terry. He knew too much about diamonds for safety.

'No ... no!. When Mrs. P. came in, he was busy with a client.'

'Okay. He mustn't know, Sydney. In fact, no one must know, or Tom will get to hear about it. Strictly speaking, this deal should go through the firm. Tom would have reason to complain if he knew what we are planning to do.'

Sydney again shifted uneasily. He knew this as well as I did.

'If I buy the necklace with my own money,' he said a little defiantly, 'it is nothing to do with Tom.'

'But Mrs. P. is a client of the firm,' I pointed out. I wanted to give him a guilt complex. 'Now look, Sydney, so as to keep the firm out of it, you had better design the collar at home and not at the office. If I get the necklace you had better keep it at home and not at the office.'

He wasn't to know it, but this was vital to my plan.

He didn't hesitate.

'Yes ... we'll keep it strictly between ourselves.' He looked trustingly at me. 'You will help with the collar, Larry?'

He had a goddamn nerve, I thought. He knew, without me he couldn't make the collar nor persuade Mrs. P. to part with her necklace at this outrageous price, yet he was planning to make himself an enormous profit, keeping Tom Luce out of it and only offering me a miserable two per cent.

'You know you can rely on me,' I said.

During the flight in the air-taxi and while thinking how I could steal the necklace in safety, I kept having qualms about Sydney because if my plan worked, he had to be the loser, but now he was showing his greed, my qualms vanished.

If he had said to me, 'Look, Larry, let's split fifty-fifty. You do all the work and I'll put up the capital,' I wouldn't have gone through with it, but as he was so goddamn greedy and selfish, only offering me two per cent, I there and then made up my mind to go ahead with my plan. He now didn't give a damn about twisting Mrs. P.'s arm, so why should I care about twisting his?

The scene I had with Mrs. P. is best forgotten. She didn't actually call Sydney a thief, but she implied it. She wept and wrung her fat hands. She stormed around the big lounge, making herself look ridiculous. She accused me of lying, reminding me that I had told her diamonds lived for ever and never lost their value. To this I reminded her the necklace would have to be broken up, and if she could wait for a year or so I would get at least a million and a half for the diamonds and platinum, but as she wanted the money at once this was the best Sydney could do.

Finally, she calmed down. After all, three-quarters of a million dollars when it isn't your loss isn't to be sneezed at. She hadn't thought that if we tried to sell the necklace as it was, there would be publicity, and this finally brought her to heel.

She said she would accept the cheque I had ready which Sydney had given me, but she added she would never deal with Luce & Fremlin again.

I made the usual tactful remarks, but I couldn't care less.

Then she came up with something so unexpected that for a long moment it threw me.

'The least you can do is to give me the glass necklace,' she said. 'It's the least you can do! If ever my husband wants to see the necklace I can show him the imitation. He won't know the difference.'

She wasn't to know, of course, but the glass necklace was the pivot on which my plan revolved. Without it, my plan to make myself two million dollars just didn't exist.

After Sydney had delivered the genuine necklace to Mrs. P., five years ago, he had asked me about the glass replica.

There was a mean streak in Sydney, and he hated wasting a dollar. I said it was in the safe and what about it? He asked if I couldn't send it back to Chan and get a rebate on it? Would Chan give us a credit for it . . . a possible three thousand dollars? What did we want with a glass replica?

The necklace had been a creation of which I was proud. I had had some luck on the stock market at the time and was feeling wealthy. I said I would return the replica to Chan and ask him what he would offer, but I didn't do that. I kept the necklace as a souvenir. When Sydney asked what had happened, I said Chan had paid me two thousand five hundred dollars for it, and I gave him my personal cheque.

Now, here was Mrs. P. asking for the replica.

After a moment, I said that it had been broken up and the stones used for other mock-ups.

She nearly blew her stack at hearing this and insisted that we should get another imitation made at once. I said I would, of course, arrange this for her, but she must realise this would take at least three months. She had to be content with that.

We went together in her Rolls to her bank, and she got the necklace from the safe deposit bank. It was in a plush leather box lined with black velvet. I hadn't seen the necklace for some four years. Its beauty made me draw in a sharp breath. I handed her the cheque, and she handed me the necklace.

She nearly fell up the stairs from the vault to pay the cheque in. I left her talking to the manager and took a taxi back to my apartment.

I unlocked my wall safe and took out the glass necklace. I laid the replica and the genuine necklaces side by side on the table and studied them.

Sydney was strictly a designer. He was no diamond expert, and I was sure he wouldn't know which was which. Chan had done a marvellous job, even Terry might be fooled until he examined the stones, then, of course, he would know, but Terry wasn't having the chance of examining them. I had taken care of that hurdle.

I put the glass necklace into the leather case and the genuine necklace into the plastic case which I put in my safe.

Then I called Sydney at the shop. I told him everything was fine. He buzzed as usual like a bee trapped in a bottle, said for me to meet him at his penthouse in half an hour.

Sydney's penthouse was magnificent. It overlooked the sea. It had a vast living-room, tastefully decorated, four bedrooms, a swimming pool on the terrace, a fountain in the hall and all the gimmicks a rich queer knew how to use.

He was waiting for me as I arrived.

'How did she take it?' he wanted to know, leading me into the big room, eyeing the brown paper parcel I was carrying.

'As you might expect. She didn't exactly call you a thief, but that's what she implied. She said she would never darken our doors again.'

Sydney sighed.

'I thought the poor thing might react that way. Well, we must be brave about it. After all, she hasn't spent anything with us for the past few years.' He continued to stare at the parcel. 'Is that it?'

This was the moment. I moved into a patch of sunlight, stripped off the brown paper and opened the case. The sunlight gave a sparkle to the glass, and Sydney gaped at the necklace.

'It's marvellous, Larry! It really is marvellous! Clever you! And now, I must get down to work.' He took the case from me, looked again at the necklace, then closed the case. The first, most important test seemed to have succeeded.

'I'll get out some designs and then we'll discuss them. I've got the week-end ahead of me.'

'That reminds me, Sydney, I've left my car at Luceville. I'll fly up there tomorrow and bring it back. Okay for me to take Monday off?'

'Of course! I'll have something we can work on by then.' I watched him walk over to a Picasso, take it down and open the wall safe which the picture concealed. I knew this safe. It was highly complicated and sophisticated: not the kind of safe you can get into without getting a load of law in your lap. He put the case into the safe, shut the safe and rehung the picture. He beamed at me. 'Keep Tuesday evening free, Larry. Come here. We'll have a little supper together and then we can go over my designs ... say at eight o'clock?'

'Fine. Okay, Sydney, I'll get back to the shop.'

On the way back, sitting in a taxi, I thought in less than twenty-four hours I would be seeing Rhea.

SIX

Soon after 1100, I pulled up outside the Morgans' bungalow. The front door stood open, but otherwise there was no sign of life.

Leaving the car, I walked across the rough grass and paused to look into the sitting-room.

Rhea was sitting at the table, a newspaper spread out before her. She looked up, her green eyes quizzing.

The sight of her brought back this tormenting lust I had for her. God! I thought, this is a woman! The most exciting, the most devilish, the most desirable woman in the world! She had on the same cheap cotton dress and the same cheap blue beads and she looked the symbol of decadent lust.

'You?' She leaned back in the chair. 'What do you want, Cheapie?'

This insane rage I couldn't control surged up in me. I took three quick steps forward and slapped her face, sending her jerking back.

'Don't call me that!' I shouted at her, and braced myself, expecting her to jump to her feet and fly at me, but she didn't. She sat still, her hands against her face, her eyes wide with surprise.

'Nice work, buster,' Fel said as he lounged into the room. 'That's the way to treat the bitch. I guessed we'd be seeing you before long. Make yourself at home.'

I ignored him, my eyes on Rhea.

'You ever touch me again and you'll be sorry,' she said, but there was no conviction in her voice. As my rage began to die down, I had a sudden idea that I had been handling her

101

wrongly with my pleading and grovelling. I remembered how her brother had slapped her around. Maybe she respected a man who got tough with her.

'You call me Cheapie again and you'll get slapped again,' I said, pushing by Fel, I sat down in the ruined armchair. 'I've come to talk to you two. Maybe if you have enough guts, we three could steal some diamonds.'

Rhea stared at me as if she thought I was crazy, but Fel burst into a loud laugh.

'You see? I told you he had spunk, you stupid cow,' he said to Rhea, 'and you wouldn't believe me. I told you he was okay. I know ... I can spot 'em a mile off.'

'Shut up!' Rhea snapped at him, still staring at me. 'Just what do you mean by that?'

'Although I have some money,' I said, 'I haven't enough ... who has? You two want money, so why not team up with me and make some?'

Her eyes glittering, her face set, she leaned forward.

'How?'

'You took the trouble to find out who I am,' I said, 'so I have taken the trouble to find out who you are. I know you have been in two crappy little hold-ups and you drew four and four. Small-time stuff. If you and your brother can think big enough and have the nerve, there's a half a million in it for you.'

Fel drew in his breath with a sharp, hissing sound, while Rhea stiffened, her hands turning into fists.

'You mean that? Half a million?' Fel asked, his voice a croak.

'I'm not here to waste time. I mean it. Half a million to you two: half a million to me.'

'You don't con me,' Rhea said harshly. 'Just what's behind this crap? You don't imagine you can kid me with this baloney, do you? I wasn't born yesterday! Half a million! Phooey!'

'Aw, rest your goddamn mouth!' Fel shouted at her. 'It's you who's a bag of baloney! I tell you this guy's okay! He's dealing it off the top deck!' He turned to me. 'Tell me more, mister ... don't bother with her, She's always had a tiny mind. What's this about half a million? Jesus! Could I use bread like that!'

'It's there for the taking,' I said. 'All you have to do is to walk in, pick it up and walk out again.'

'You mean walk into that store of yours and clean it out?' Fel said, puzzled.

'Don't talk like an idiot! If you tried that you'd be in jail so fast you wouldn't know what had hit you. No ... this job is easy, safe and simple.'

'And what do you do?' Rhea broke in, her eyes suspicious and cold. 'Stand on the side-lines while we do the work and if the job turns sour, you duck out of sight?'

'Nothing can go wrong. It's simple,' I said. 'I organise the job and sell the diamonds. Without me, there's no money. But if you haven't the guts to do it, say so now and I'll find some-one else to do it.'

'Man! Hasn't this guy changed since last he was here!' There was a note of awe in Fel's voice. 'What's got into you, mister?'

'You two have got into me,' I said. 'You started me think-ing.' I looked at Rhea. 'I've decided not to wait to become old, fat and stupid. I've decided to become rich now.'

Still her eyes were suspicious.

'So what's the job?' she asked, frowning at me, but I knew I had caught her interest. 'Don't talk in circles. What's it all about?'

I had come prepared. I took from my wallet a photograph of Mrs. P.'s necklace and laid it on the table in front of her.

'That's what it's all about: one million, eight hundred thou-sand dollars worth of diamonds.'

Fel came to lean over his sister's shoulder. I watched them, and by the sudden greed on their faces I knew I had hooked them as I had hooked Sydney.

Then Rhea looked up at me.

'We could go away for twenty years if this one turned sour.'

'Hell!' Fel exploded. 'Can't you stop griping? Must you always try to throw a goddamn spanner in the works? Why don't you shut up?'

'I've been in jail ... you haven't,' she said. 'You talk like the moron you are.'

'There won't be any jail,' I put in. 'Let me explain.'

I then told them about Mrs. P.'s necklace, showed them the newspaper cuttings and the press photos of her wearing the necklace. I told them how she was in the hole for thousands because of her gambling and how she had to sell the necklace secretly. How my boss had bought it at a knock-down price and how he and I were going to make the diamonds into a collar and sell it at a big profit.

'The mean sonofabitch is only offering me two per cent of the take,' I concluded, 'so I'm going to take the necklace. In my position I can sell the stones safely for a million. I'll split fifty-fifty with you two,' and using Sydney's pet phrase, I went on, 'I can't be fairer than that, can I?'

Rhea studied me.

'You're damned generous, aren't you?' Her cold suspicious eyes searched my face. 'What's the idea? You know we'd have done it for a tenth of that price. What's the idea?'

I realised then that I had over-played my hand. She was right, of course. If I had offered them fifty thousand, they would still have jumped at it, but it was too late now to back track. I had made a slip and now I had to lull her suspicions. Keeping my face expressionless, I met her steady stare with one as steady.

'The way I see it,' I said, 'as you two do the dangerous part of the job and I pay you half, you won't be dissatisfied and you'll keep your mouths shut. The last thing I want is for you to try to blackmail me for more money when the job's done. To take care of that and to safeguard myself, I'm splitting the take down the middle.'

'This guy thinks ahead ... he uses his nut,' Fel said excitedly. 'You're right, mister. With half a million you won't ever hear from us again!'

'The dangerous part of the job?' Rhea was quick to pounce on yet another slip. 'You said it was simple and easy. So where's the danger come in?'

'I should have said the active part of the job, not dangerous, but there's bound to be tension.' I was telling myself I had to be more careful with her. Whereas her brother was a gullible fool, she was as tricky as a sack full of rattlesnakes.

She continued to stare at me for a long moment, then finally, she asked, 'So what do we do?'

'First, make yourselves look respectable: a brother and sister on vacation. Buy some respectable-looking clothes with the money you stole from me. Then you come to Paradise City and put up at the Pyramid Motel: register as John and Mary Hall.' I took out my gold pencil and wrote my telephone number on the margin of the newspaper lying on the table. 'Call me Tuesday night after midnight and give me the number of your cabin. I don't want to ask for you at the reception desk. On Wednesday night I'll come to your cabin at ten o'clock with all the details you'll need. You could do the job next Friday, but I'll let you know for certain when we meet on Wednesday.'

'You still haven't told us how we do the job,' Rhea said, watching me. 'I want to know.'

'My boss and I will be working on the design for the collar at his penthouse, and the necklace will be on his desk. We need it for the new design. All you have to do is to walk in, tie us up so we can't raise the alarm, pick up the necklace and walk out. It's as easy and as simple as that.'

'Well, for Pete's sake!' Fel exclaimed. 'You mean it really will be as easy as that? No fuzz to worry about? We just walk in and take the goddamn thing?'

'That's it.' I got to my feet. 'Any further questions?'

'We've got to have guns?' Fel asked.

'Of course, but not loaded. There'll be no opposition. Just use them as a threat . . . you understand? Not loaded.'

'Sure. I can get hold of a couple of rods okay.'

'We'll go into details next Wednesday. Leave the organising to me. All you have to do is to get yourselves decent-looking outfits, look respectable and don't attract attention.' I looked at Rhea. 'Have you any questions?'

She studied me, frowning.

'What's the catch?' she asked. 'That's my question. This job stinks to me: half a million bucks; simple, dead easy and no fuzz. It stinks! What's your game?'

I turned to Fel.

'Do you think you can find someone to work with you? I'm getting sick of her. After all two men are better than a man and a suspicious bitch.'

He grinned.

'Pay no attention to her. She always runs at the mouth. We'll be at the motel Tuesday night, mister.'

'If I don't hear from you by midnight Tuesday, I'll know you haven't the guts to do the job and I'll look elsewhere.'

I made that my exit line.

During the five years I had worked for Sydney I had been to his penthouse scores of times. The nightman, Bert Lawson, knew me and always had a cheery salute for me when he let me in.

At 2200 the glass door to the entrance lobby was locked. Once the door was locked, Lawson retired to his little office and spent the rest of the night watching TV. He only appeared to let in the occasional visitor and to answer the telephone which rarely disturbed him.

The four rich occupants, including Sydney, had their keys to the entrance door and let themselves in after 2200. Apart from Sydney, the other three were elderly and seldom if ever went out at night. This made it easy for me. The lock on the entrance door was a Yale. Lawson pressed down the catch at locking up time and then the door could only be opened by a key. I didn't anticipate any trouble when coming to see Sydney after 2200. Lawson would let me in. I would take the elevator to the top floor, then walk down to the lobby. By that time, Lawson would be back in his office, watching TV. All I had to do would be to sneak across the lobby, put up the catch, then walk up the stairs to Sydney's penthouse.

Sydney also had a Yale lock on his front door. As he was always forgetting his keys, he seldom kept his front door locked, knowing the entrance door to the apartment block was always guarded during the day and locked at night. If, on the night of the raid, he did happen to lock his door when I was with him, I could find an excuse to unlock it. I could leave my brief-case in the lobby, come out to fetch it while he was working at his desk, slip the catch, unlocking the door. It was essential that Rhea and Fel should rush into the penthouse and take Sydney by surprise. I was sure he would collapse with fright. At the sight of a gun, he would shrivel. I was sure I would have no trouble from him, but to keep suspicion off me, I would have to act brave. I would have to be pistol whipped by Fel. I didn't like this idea, but it was essential to keep me clear of any suspicion. I had already suffered concussion from the air crash. He mustn't hit me over the head, I told myself, but across the face.

All these thoughts were going through my head as I drove back to Paradise City. I felt reasonably convinced that both Rhea and Fel were hooked in spite of Rhea's suspicions. But if they imagined I would let them walk off with one million eight hundred thousands dollars worth of diamonds they were in for another think.

The trick in my plan was to let them steal the glass necklace. During the flight back to Paradise City in the air taxi, I had begun to realise I was getting misgivings about Rhea. Now, driving back in the Buick I asked myself if I really wanted to have an association with her. I lusted for her, but discovered I was lusting for a million dollars more than her. If I could have laid her like the whore she was, I would have done it, but seeing her this time warned me she was hard, tough and ruthless, without a spark of feeling in her. As I drove mile after mile, I began to come around to the idea of using her and her brother as my cat's paws. Unlike her moron of a brother, she was suspicious of me. I would now have to be very careful how I handled her on Wednesday night.

It would be a complete let-down if, like some wild cat, sniffing at a concealed trap and knowing instinctively that it was a trap, she wouldn't do the job. Without her and Fel the plan was abortive. I had no other connections with the underworld. I couldn't ask around for two men to pull a jewel robbery.

So everything depended on how I handled her on Wednesday night. I was sure she would come to the motel, but by then, she would have had time to think and to search for snags and to try to find out why I had stupidly offered half a million. From the expression in her cold, green eyes, I was sure she hadn't been convinced by my explanation.

But I was certain of one thing: it would never occur to her that the necklace was a fake. I felt, since I was willing to let them take the necklace, her suspicions would be lulled. Letting them take the necklace was the bait in the trap and I was confident such a bait wouldn't occur to her. Surely she would feel she had the whip hand with the necklace in her possession. She would be sure that I couldn't double-cross her.

When I arrived at the shop on Tuesday morning, Jane Bowman, my secretary, told me that Sydney wouldn't be in. He was feeling unwell. I guessed he was struggling with the design of the collar and it was proving difficult. I wondered if I should telephone him, but with Terry watching me, I decided I would call him during my lunch time.

Business was brisk that morning. I sold a diamond clip, a bracelet and an engagement ring before I went to lunch.

Using a call booth, I spoke to Sydney. He sounded depressed.

'Larry, precious, this isn't going to be easy. I've tried and tried over the week-end and I'm getting just a wee bit desperate.'

This was unlike Sydney, but I knew his task would be difficult.

'Two million dollars are never easy to make, Sydney,' I said. 'Have you anything to show me tonight?'

'Show you?' His voice went up into a squeak. 'Hundreds and hundreds of designs I'm sick of looking at them.'

'Don't worry. I'll be around at nine and we'll sort them out ... okay?'

'You do sound so confident! Yes ... I'll get Claude to cook a beautiful dinner ... come earlier. Come at eight.'

108

'Sorry, I'm tied up. I'll see you at nine,' and I hung up.

I wanted our meetings during the time we were working on the collar to be late. This was essential to my plan.

Claude, Sydney's Man Friday, was a fat, kindly queer who once had been an under chef at Maxim's of Paris. His working hours were from 0800 to 2200. He arrived promptly and left promptly. His cooking was superlative and he kept Sydney's luxury home immaculate with the help of two coloured women to do the rough work.

That evening, a few minutes after 2100, he opened the door to my ring and beamed at me. I was one of his rare favourites.

'Good evening, Mr. Larry. May I say how glad I am that you are better?' His greeting was genuine. 'Do go in. Mr. Sydney is expecting you.' Lowering his voice, he went on, 'Dinner is nearly ready so please don't linger too long over the cocktails.'

I said I would take care of that and then went into the vast living-room where I found Sydney at his desk, a treble dry martini at his side.

'Larry! How glad I am to see you ... this is utter hell! Come and look!'

I went over to the big cocktail shaker and poured myself a large martini, then dropped into one of the big lounging chairs.

'Not now, Sydney. Let's eat first. We have the night before us.'

'My head is simply buzzing.' Sydney carried his glass to another chair near mine and sat down. 'I'm beginning to wonder if this is going to work. God! I couldn't sleep last night! I kept thinking I've given that dreadful woman three-quarters of a million! I must be out of my tiny mind! I am beginning to wonder if I'll ever get my money back!'

'Relax ... you'll get it back plus. Now don't get in a tizz, Sydney. We'll sort it out after dinner.' Although I could see he wasn't interested, I went on to tell him of the happenings in the shop, what I had sold, who had bought and how a lot of people had asked for him.

Talking in this way, I finished my martini as Claude an-

109

nounced dinner was served. It was an exceptionally excellent meal: stuffed gulls' eggs, followed by *noisette d'agneau Edward VII*, one of Maxim's great specialities.

After dinner, we returned to the living-room. I heard Claude let himself out and the front door clicked to. I wondered if he had left the catch down.

'I'm just going to visit the small room,' I said, 'then let's get at it.'

As Sydney sat at his desk, I went into the lobby, saw the catch was up and the door unlocked, then I went into the toilet, lifted the flush plug and returned to the living-room.

We spent the next half-hour going through Sydney's designs. This was to me a waste of time knowing there would be no collar, but I had to act out the play. Among the many designs, I selected three which I said were getting very near the idea.

'Do you really think so, Larry? You're not just being kind?' Sydney looked anxiously at me.

'Are you working with the necklace at your side?'

'Why, no.' His eyes popped open. 'I keep it in the safe.'

'That's it!' I snapped my fingers. 'That's why you're having this trouble. Get the necklace and put it on your desk. You'll get inspiration from it.'

He stared at me, then a happy smile lit up his face.

'You know I never thought of that! Clever you? You could be so right!' He went through the performance of removing the Picasso and opening the safe. Even though I knew he trusted me utterly, he kept his body between me and the safe so I couldn't see how he opened it. He had spent a lot of money on the safe and how it was opened was his secret and for no one else.

He put the necklace on the desk. I shifted his desk light so the light fell directly on the glass imitations. They certainly looked good.

He sat down and stared at the necklace for some minutes, then he picked up the best of his designs and examined it.

'You're right, Larry, precious. I've got the wrong gradation here. Silly me! Yes, I think I can do better than this.' He began to sketch feverishly while I smoked, watching him. In half an hour, after three unsuccessful attempts, he produced a rough that was so impressive I felt that if I didn't curb his enthusiasm a second meeting wouldn't be necessary and there had to be a second meeting.

'This is it! I feel it!' he exclaimed excitedly. 'Look!'

It was of course exactly right.

'It's good,' I said but made my voice sound flat.

'It's right! You see how I've placed the big stone? Why didn't I think of that before?'

'It's excellent.' I frowned, then shook my head.

'Don't you think it's right?' he asked anxiously.

'Nearly right. I could sell this for a million and a half, but we want two million.'

'I'm not buying any more stones.' Sydney's voice turned petulant, 'if that's what you're thinking.'

'No ... no, of course not. The arrangement is perfect. I'm not sure about the setting. Maybe it's too classical. We mustn't rush this Sydney. Let me think about it. I'll come here on Friday night. By then I'm sure we'll have come up with the solution.'

'Friday night?' He opened his engagement diary and consulted it. 'Not Friday. I have a dreary dinner date I just can't break. Thursday would be all right.'

'Fine.' I got to my feet. I was telling myself I had all day Wednesday and all Thursday until 2200 to tie up any loose ends ... it should be enough time. 'I'll be here just after ten o'clock. Then the next move is Hong Kong.'

'Come earlier, Larry. Claude will prepare something special for you.'

'I'm sorry. I can't come earlier. I'm having dinner with the Johnsons (a lie) ... God held me! She's interested in a diamond clip. When I know more or less what she wants, I'll ask you to get some designs out for her.'

'That dreadful old biddy!' Sydney sighed. 'Always the old and the fat.'

'They have the money.'

I put his design in my wallet.

'How are you feeling, Larry? You still look peaky,' Sydney asked as he accompanied me to the front door.

'All right. I get tired. When we've sold this collar, I think it might be an idea to go on a cruise ... if it would be all right with you.'

'You sell this collar, precious, and you can go to the moon if you want to and I'll pick up the tab.'

When he had shut the front door, I paused to listen. He didn't slip the catch.

Things seemed to be going my way.

I returned to my apartment at 2320. Mixing myself a whisky and soda, I sat down and took stock.

Assuming Rhea and Fel were hooked and would do the job, I felt confident they could get into the apartment block and into Sydney's penthouse without trouble.

I remembered Rhea had a record. She must wear gloves. If she left one fingerprint, my plan would blow up in my face for I felt certain if they were caught, they would give me away.

But would the police come into it?

Sydney's position was tricky. If he called the police, then Plessington would learn his wife had sold the necklace. Sydney might not care about that, but he certainly would care if his partner, Tom Luce, got to hear about it. This might cause an irreparable rift between them for Sydney knew, as I knew, he was behaving unethically. Luce was tough and he wouldn't easily forgive Sydney and this, I knew Sydney would want to avoid at all costs. Tom was even more important to him than my expertise.

But would Sydney be prepared to kiss three-quarters of a million goodbye without doing anything about it? Although I knew he was immensely rich, to lose a sum that big would be crippling. After some thought I decided he might do just that rather than face Tom Luce's wrath and also the damage Mrs. P. could do, going around to all his wealthy clients, saying he wasn't to be trusted. If he didn't think of this, then I would point it out to him.

If he didn't call the police, then I was in the clear. I would sell the necklace stone by stone, stash the money away in

Switzerland, continue to work for Sydney for three or four months, then plead ill-health and resign. I would then go to Europe and settle down somewhere, probably in the Swiss Alps with my million dollars.

Then I remembered Rhea and Fel. How would they react when they discovered they had stolen glass and not diamonds? Those two could be as dangerous and as vicious as Spooky. Being involved in the robbery, they wouldn't dare inform on me, but they could come after me.

I brooded about this. Then I remembered I would have to be pistol whipped by Fel to keep suspicion from me. I would take advantage of this. I could make out that my nerves had been shot to hell and I had to get away at once. By the way I would fix it, it would take Rhea and Fel some ten days before they found out they had stolen an imitation. By that time I would be in Europe and far away from their avenging hands. Then I would write to Sydney, telling him I was quitting for good.

I sat there, nursing my drink, my mind busy when at three minutes past midnight, the telephone bell rang.

My hand wasn't too steady as I lifted the receiver.

'Carr here.'

Fel said, 'Cabin 35.'

I drew in a deep breath.

'She there?'

Fel chuckled.

'You bet.'

'Tomorrow night at ten,' I said and hung up.

The following day dragged interminably. Fortunately, we were not busy in the shop and I could do some thinking.

Terry had been watching me. Finally, he became curious and he sauntered over to my desk.

'Have you something on your mind, Larry?' he asked, staring at me with his mean little eyes. 'You seem awfully thoughtful.'

'A headache,' I said briefly, jumping at the chance to make out I was still far from well.

'So sorry.' He looked as sorry as a man who finds a ten dollar bill in the street. 'You returned too soon. I can't understand why Sydney wanted you back so badly. There are times when he is so inconsiderate. I was quite capable of handling your work as well as mine. Why don't you go home and nurse your poor head? Miss Barlow and I can manage beautifully.'

I was on the point of telling him to go to hell when I realised as part of my act, I'd better make out I was feeling pretty bad.

'I think I will.' I got to my feet. 'If you really think you can manage.'

I could see by the surprised expression in his eyes, he hadn't expected this. With Sydney still away and now me going, he certainly would have to pick up his feet.

But this was a challenge he gladly accepted. As I walked to the parking lot I wondered how Sydney was getting on with the design of the setting. I felt I had to tell him I was going to take it easy at home. I spoke to him from a call booth.

'Sydney, I have a hell of a headache. Terry says he can manage so I'm going home.'

'You poor thing! Do that.' He began to buzz. 'I'll get down there right away ... can't possibly leave Terry in charge. I've got four lovely designs. You'll be so pleased! You wouldn't like to come around tonight?'

'I'd rather not. I'll take it easy for today if you don't mind.'

'You do that.'

I didn't immediately return to my apartment. I went to my bank and got $3,000 in Traveller's cheques. Then I went to my travel agent and inquired about planes to San Francisco. There was one leaving Friday morning at 0500. I made a note and asked if reservations were necessary. My travel agent said the flight, at that time, would be half empty and I could walk on: no problem.

I returned to my apartment, sat down and really got down to planning the steal. I sent out for sandwiches at lunch time and by 1500, I was satisfied I had taken care of all the details.

Sydney called at 1600 to inquire how I felt. I said the headache had gone away, but I still felt a bit shaky.

He inquired anxiously if I thought I'd be all right for Thursday night and I said I would and I'd be at my desk tomorrow at the usual time.

At 2000, I went around the corner to a little restaurant and had a light meal, then I returned to my apartment and tried to watch TV until 2145. Taking the sling bag containing the Beatle wig, the silver glasses, the red jacket with the black patched pockets, but leaving the toy gun, I went down to the garage and drove out to the Pyramid Motel. I had chosen this motel for the Morgans to stay at because it had separate cabins and was used by young people travelling through to Miami. If Rhea and Fel had bought the right clothes they would be just two in a crowd.

I parked the car outside the motel and walked in. I had no trouble in finding cabin 35. Each cabin carried a big illuminated sign, showing its number.

The night air was strident with the sound of transistors and squawking voices from TVs. There was no one to see me knock on the door of cabin 35, which opened immediately as if Fel had been waiting impatiently. I entered the room and Fel shut the door.

For a moment I didn't recognise Rhea as she stood by the table, looking at me with her cold, green eyes. She had on a blood-red trouser suit with white collar and cuffs. Her red hair was piled to the top of her head instead of hanging to her shoulders, and it had been washed. The sight of her again sent a stab of lust through me and I knew she knew it by her sneering little smile. I turned to look at Fel. Even he had managed to make himself look respectable. He had had his hair cut and was wearing a brown sports jacket and a pair of bottle green slacks. A white polo collar sweater completed his outfit.

'You two look fine,' I said, putting the sling bag on the table. 'Have you got another change of clothes?'

'Yeah. We reckoned this gear would be easy to describe to the cops,' Fell said, grinning. 'We go hippy after the job.'

Well, at least they were using their heads, I thought.

115

I went around the table and sat down.

'Since you're both here, I take it the operation is on ... right?'

'We're here to listen,' Rhea said woodenly. 'Tell us the whole operation, then we'll make up our minds.'

I was expecting this and shrugged.

'The operation is on tomorrow night.'

'Tomorrow night?' Fel's voice shot up. 'That's rushing it, isn't it?'

'What does it matter if it's tomorrow night or next week? I have it all organised. The sooner it is done, the faster we get the money.'

Fel looked over at Rhea.

'Let him talk,' she said and sat down, away from me and lit a cigarette.

'Tomorrow night at exactly 1030, you arrive at Wellington Court, Roosevelt Boulevard.' I took from my wallet a sheet of folded paper and put it on the table. 'I've written it all down for you with directions how to get there. Tomorrow morning, take a look at the place: just drive past so you're sure of finding it. Time your run from here to Wellington Court so you will know when to leave here tomorrow night. At that time of night there will be vacant parking bays close by. Leave your car, walk casually to the front entrance. You will find the door unlocked. Go quickly up the stairs. Don't use the elevator. The nightman will be in his office watching TV but the elevator just might cause interference on the screen, so use the stairs. When you reach the top floor, turn right and you will see Fremlin's front door ... No. 4. The door will be unlocked. Open it silently and go in. You will find yourselves in a small lobby, facing the door, leading into the sitting-room. Listen outside the door. You will hear Fremlin and me talking. Then rush in. Come in really fast, guns in hand and yell at us to stay still. You don't have to worry about Fremlin. He'll just sit there, goggling at you, terrified. Now, here is the trickiest part of the operation.' I turned to look at Fel who was sitting with his elbows on his knees, his face in his hands, listening with intense concentration. 'I have to act brave. This should shift any

116

suspicion from me that I'm connected with the steal, and this is essential if I'm to sell the diamonds. I will jump to my feet and come at you. You will side-swipe me across the face with your gun.'

Fel gaped at me.

'A bang across the face with a gun can hurt,' he said.

'I know that, but it's got to be done and done convincingly. I'm not going to moan if I lose a tooth. A million is a lot of money.'

'You really mean you want me to bash you with the gun?'

'Across the face: not the head. I want to get that clear. Not the head: across the face. Do you understand?'

'Why not save your looks, mister and take a rap on the nut?' Fel asked, frowning.

'I've had concussion. It would be dangerous to hit me over the head.'

'Yeah.' Again he looked at Rhea, but she sat still, her face expressionless, her eyes watchful.

'I fall down,' I went on. 'You two take care of Sydney. Bring with you a roll of two-inch tape. Bind and gag him. Do the same to me. You will find the necklace on the desk. Take it and get out.' I paused, then went on, 'That the operation. It's straightforward. There will be no opposition, no police and if you've taped us well enough, we will have to wait until Fremlin's manservant arrives at eight in the morning to release us.' I lit a cigarette, then asked, 'Any questions so far?'

'You want to ask him anything?' Fel asked Rhea. 'It's fine with me.'

'Not yet.' She flicked ash on the carpet. 'Keep talking,' she said to me.

'You have to have an alibi,' I went on. 'Your story is you left Luceville on Monday afternoon for a trip to 'Frisco. Rhea thought she might get a job there and you drove her up. This will account for your bungalow being shut up for two days and on the night of the robbery. Rhea will catch the 0500 flight on Friday morning to 'Frisco. You, Fel, will drive flat out back to Luceville the moment the robbery is over. You should get there Friday night. Tell anyone interested that Rhea has gone to 'Frisco after a job. The chances are you won't need an alibi, but you have to have one just in case.'

'Yeah.' Fel nodded. 'That makes sense.'

I took from my billfold the Traveller's cheques and tossed them into Rhea's lap.

'This will take care of your expenses. There's no trouble getting an air ticket to 'Frisco; give a phoney name and address. At that hour you walk on. Stay at a modest hotel and look for work. This is important in case the police check. Then after ten days, come back to Luceville ... not sooner ... you understand? ... ten days.'

She now asked her first question.

'So what happens to the necklace? Do we stuff it in your pocket before we scram so you can sell it?'

'If you think that's a hot idea with Sydney watching, you need your head examined,' I said, now very alert. 'You take the necklace with you. Either you take it or Fel takes it and hides it in the bungalow. That's up to you.'

She stared at me, her eyes narrowing.

'You're pretty trustful, aren't you? Suppose we take off with the necklace. You'd look dumb, wouldn't you?'

'Suppose you did that?' I smiled at her. 'Do you imagine you could sell it? It will have to be broken up. Okay, so you break it up. We are in this for a million. You would have an impossible job to find any fence to handle it and if he did he'd rob you blind. That's why I can afford to trust you. I know dealers who will pay me the highest prices for these stones and no questions asked ... you don't. It's as simple as that.'

She considered this, then for the first time she began to relax.

'So okay,' she said, 'but what happens when you sell the stones? You take the necklace. So suppose you run off with it and leave us looking dumb?'

She was following the pattern of my past thinking. I had anticipated she would ask this and I was ready for her.

'Fel goes back to the bungalow to keep up appearances,' I said, 'but you come along as my secretary. You'll be in on all the deals. You'll know what I'm getting paid for each individual stone. I'll be paid in cash. As each stone is paid for I'll give you half of what I get. Does that assure you you won't be double-crossed?'

She sat back, staring at me. I had cut the ground from under her feet. She couldn't think of any other objections.

'Just so long as you don't walk out on me when I'm not looking.'

Again I smiled at her.

'I won't have the chance even if I wanted to. The idea is we stick close together,' I paused, then went on, looking directly at her, 'we even sleep together . . . that's part of the bargain.'

Fel gave a guffaw of laughter.

'This guy's my man! Brother! You deserve what you get!'

Rhea suddenly smiled: a hard, cold smile, but still a smile.

'You have yourself a deal,' she said. 'Okay, we'll do the job.'

I drew a long deep breath.

'Right. Now let's settle the remaining details and then I'll get home. First, you both wear gloves. This is vitally important. If you leave just one fingerprint in Fremlin's penthouse there won't be any million.' I waved to the sling bag. 'I've brought along an outfit for Fel. Take a look.'

Fel opened the bag and took out the wig, the glasses and the jacket. Grinning he put on the wig and the glasses and surveyed himself in the mirror.

'Man! This is super! I don't even recognise myself!'

I looked at Rhea.

'Hide your hair under a scarf. Get yourself a pair of those glasses to hide your green eyes. As soon as the job's over, change out of the things you're now wearing. Get a cheap suitcase, put your things in it and dump it somewhere safe. Fel will have to do that . . . understand?'

She nodded. She was much less hostile now and I knew I had her hooked.

I tapped the paper on the table.

'It's all written down here,' I said. 'Everything I've told you. Go over it and over it until you know every move by heart, then destroy it.' I got to my feet. 'I guess that's all.

Tomorrow night at ten-thirty.' I again looked at Fel. 'Remember my face and not my head. Hit me hard enough to look convincing.'

He grimaced.

'Rather you than me.'

I paused at the door to look at them.

'Rather me than a million dollars,' I said and left them.

SEVEN

Thursday passed off as well as could be expected. I was edgy in spite of trying not to be and Sydney drove me nearly crazy with his buzzing and fluttering. He kept appearing from his office, spinning around the showroom, giving me conspiratorial looks and then buzzing back out of sight. Of course, Terry became aware that something was cooking and he watched me with baleful, curious eyes.

Finally, I decided this must stop. I went into his office, closing the door.

'For Pete's sake, Sydney,' I said, 'do control yourself. You're behaving like an escapee from the Mafia.'

His eyes popped wide open.

'I am? I'm as calm as a bishop. What do you mean?'

'As calm as a bishop who finds he has a girl in his bed.'

He giggled.

'Well, maybe I am just a wee bit excited. I just can't wait for tonight! You'll be utterly thrilled!'

'Keep it for tonight and stop buzzing around me. Terry is chewing his nails with curiosity.'

He took the hint and remained in his office for the rest of the afternoon, but when he left at 1800, he couldn't resist giving me a broad wink. I frowned at him and a little crushed, he took himself off.

Terry immediately got to his feet and wandered over to me.

'What's the excitement about?' he asked. 'He's been behaving like a yo-yo all day. Are you two cooking up something?'

I began to clear my desk.

'Why not ask him? If he wants you to know, he'll surely tell you.'

Terry put his hands on my desk and leaned forward. His mean little eyes were furious.

'You hate me, don't you?'

I stood up.

'No more than you hate me, Terry,' I said and went across the showroom to the washroom.

Ten minutes later, I was driving back to my apartment. In a week, perhaps less, I told myself, I would be in Antwerp, talking to one of the biggest diamond buyers in the business. I would offer him ten of the best stones, but not the big one. This I was going to take to Hatton Garden, London. Wallace Bernstein had already asked me to look out for a top class stone that could be used in a tiara. He hinted it was for one of the Royal family. I had no doubt he would jump at the big stone and at my price. Then from London to Amsterdam, then to Hamburg and finally to Switzerland. By then I would be worth a million dollars. That sum invested in 8 per cent Bonds would give me an income for life of $80,000. I would apply for a Swiss *livret pour étrangers*, pay token tax and I would be set for life.

I was satisfied with the way I had handled Rhea. I was sure now that she was no longer suspicious and this was important. With her out of the way, cooling her heels in 'Frisco and Fel out of the way in Luceville, I had room in which to man-oeuvre.

A lot depended now on whether Sydney would call in the police after the robbery. I would have to be careful how I handled him. He would be in a terrible state and furiously angry. When like that he was difficult to control. I would have to warn him and keep warning him that once the police took over, Tom Luce was certain to get to hear what had happened. It depended on whether Sydney's rage or his fear of Luce won the battle and I was inclined to bet on the latter.

I got back to my apartment at 1835. I had four hours ahead of me to kill. Remembering I was supposed to be dining with the Johnsons, I took a shower, shaved and changed into a dark suit. Although I did all this in slow motion, I still had three hours and a quarter before I went into action.

I made myself a stiff whisky, turned on the TV which didn't hold me, so turned it off. I wandered up and down my living-room, uneasy and edgy. I kept looking at my watch. I didn't feel like eating. There was a sick sensation growing in my stomach, but the whisky helped. For no reason at all I suddenly thought of Jenny. I had a sudden impulse to speak to her. Searching through my pocket diary, I found the number of the city hospital, Luceville and put through a call.

After a little delay, Jenny said, 'Hello?'

'Hello yourself.' I sat down, feeling suddenly relaxed. 'This is your old partner in Welfare. How are you, Jenny?'

'Larry!' The lift in her voice made me feel good. 'How nice of you to call. I'm getting along fine now. I can even hobble around with two sticks.'

'You can ... that's wonderful! When are you leaving?'

'The end of the next week. I can't wait to get out and to get around again. Tell me, Larry, is all well with you?'

I wondered how she would react if I told her I was about to involve myself in a robbery.

'I'm all right. Back in harness again ... busy. I have a dinner date. I just finished dressing when you suddenly jumped into my mind.'

'I've been thinking of you too. I'm so glad you left this town, Larry. Luceville wasn't for you.'

'I guess. Yet I miss it ... and you.' I suddenly wanted to see her again, but I knew this wasn't possible. In four or five days I would be on my way to Europe and probably wouldn't ever come back. I thought of her untidy hair, her eyes, her efficiency and her kindness. 'I have to go to Europe in a few days ... business. Otherwise, I would have driven up to see you.'

'Oh!' A pause, then she went on, 'Will you be away long?'

'I'm not sure ... it depends. I may have to go on to Hong Kong. Yes ... it'll be some time.'

'I see ... well, have a good trip.' There was a sudden flat note in her voice that told me she was upset. I stared at the opposite wall. I thought of the loneliness that lay ahead of me.

An exile living in a foreign country ... I didn't even speak any language except my own. How different it would have been to have Jenny with me. With all that money, we could make a wonderful life together. These thoughts flashed through my mind as she said, 'I suppose the sun is shining your way. Here, it is dreadful. There are times when I long for the sun.'

I thought of the fun I would have showing her Hong Kong, then with a feeling of heavy depression I realised I had left it too late. I couldn't say 'Come away with me.' I couldn't jump it on her like that. Besides, she couldn't walk yet. No ... it was too late I would have to leave within a few days after the robbery: probably Monday next. It would be too dangerous not to leave.

'The sun's marvellous here,' I said and now wished I hadn't called her. 'I'll write, Jenny. Well, it's getting late. Look after yourself.'

'And you too.'

We spoke for a few more seconds, then I hung up. I sat there, staring at the wall. Was I in love with her? I wondered. I was beginning to think I was, but was she in love with me? Maybe when I was safe in Switzerland, I would write to her and tell her how I felt about her. I would ask her if she would come to Switzerland so we could talk about it. I would send her the air ticket. I felt she would come.

I looked at my watch: still two hours and three-quarters to wait. I couldn't stay any longer in the apartment so I left and drove to an Interflora that remained open late. I ordered roses to be sent to Jenny and wrote a card on which I said I would be in touch with her before long. Then knowing I should eat something, I drove to the Spanish Bay Hotel and went into the snack bar. I had a smoked salmon sandwich and a glass of neat vodka.

One of my clients, Jack Calshot, a rich, boozy-faced stock-broker came over and joined me. We talked of this and that. He said he was looking for an emerald and ruby bracelet and gave me a heavy wink. 'Not for the wife, you understand. I've found me a piece of tail that's really enthusiastic, but she needs softening. Got anything like that, Larry?'

I said it was no problem and for him to look in at the shop tomorrow.

I spent the next hour listening to his chat. He was a useful man to know as I had had several good market tips from him in the past. At the back of my mind I thought that very soon all this would change—yet another change of scene. I wondered if I would make friends in Switzerland. From what I had heard about the Swiss, they weren't overfriendly to foreigners, but at least there would be an American colony I could get to know.

Finally, my watch hands crawled to 2145. I said so long to Calshot who said he would be around tomorrow at ten o'clock. As I got into the Buick I thought of Fel and flinched inwardly. *A bang across the face can hurt*. A million dollars could never be easy to earn, I told myself.

As I buzzed the entrance bell to Sydney's apartment block and as Lawson came across the lobby, I saw Claude come out of the elevator.

They both greeted me as Lawson opened the door.

When Lawson had returned to his office, moving at a trot that told me he had a good show to watch on TV, Claude said, 'Mr. Sydney is very excitable this evening, Mr. Larry. I had some trouble persuading him to eat his dinner. I do hope you will have a calming influence on him.'

When I thought of what was going to happen, I decided that would be unlikely.

'I'll do my best, Claude,' I said. 'Goodnight,' and I took the elevator to the penthouse. Leaving the elevator, I started down the stairs, moving swiftly. I reached the lobby, paused, looked around, then crossing quickly to the entrance door, I turned the knob, lifted the catch, then spun around and started up the stairs. As I had thought, unlocking the entrance door had presented no problems. Reaching Sydney's front door, I gently turned the handle and found the door unlocked. I re-shut it and rang the bell.

Sydney came bounding to the door, throwing it wide open.

'Come in, dear boy!' he exclaimed, his eyes sparkling. 'Did you have a dreadful dinner?'

'Pretty bad.' I closed the front door and taking his arm, went with him into the living-room, knowing that the door was unlocked. 'She's dithering. I don't think her husband wants to spend the money, but I ran into Calshot and he's after an emerald and ruby bracelet. He'll be in tomorrow ... another new chick.'

'Never mind him ... come and look at my designs.'

As I followed him to the desk, I glanced at my watch. The time was 2210. In another twenty minutes all hell would break loose. I found I was sweating slightly, and taking out my handkerchief, I wiped my hands.

'Look!' He spread four designs out on the desk. 'What do you think?'

I bent over them, scarcely seeing them.

'Don't you think this one's marvellous?' He put his long artistically shaped finger on the second design.

I pulled myself together and forced my eyes to focus. For several seconds I examined the designs. He had surpassed himself. The second to which he had pointed was the best piece of jewellery designing I had ever seen.

I straightened.

'You're a genius, Sydney! There's no mistake about that! This is the one! It's top class and if I can't sell it for two million then my name's not Carr!'

He simpered, wriggling with pleasure.

'I thought it had to be right, but now you say so ...'

'Let's compare it with the necklace.'

He looked surprised.

'But why?'

'I want to compare the cut of the stones with your design.' I began with a husky voice and had to pause to clear my throat.

'I see ... yes ...'

He turned, crossed the room, removed the Picasso and went through his secret motions of opening the safe.

I looked at my watch: another fifteen minutes.

He brought the necklace and laid it on the desk.

'Sit down, Sydney and let's compare it.'

He went around his desk and I got behind him and we both

126

looked first at the necklace and then the design.

'It's marvellous,' I said. 'You've caught the spirit of the stones beautifully. Can you imagine how this will look after Chan has finished with it? I can't wait to get it to him.'

He swivelled around in his chair.

'When can you get off?'

'Monday. I'll see my travel man tomorrow. I should be in Hong Kong some time Wednesday. I'll have to spend a week with Chan, making sure he starts right, then I'll fly back.'

He nodded.

'That's good. How long do you think you'll take to sell it?'

'That's a toughie. I don't know. I'm already working on a list of names. Chan will take two months on this job. As soon as he's finished, I'll start.'

'You can't give me any idea?'

I stared at him, not understanding what he was getting at.

'I don't think that's possible, Sydney. It could be a month, could be eight months. Two million isn't small.'

He fidgeted on his chair.

'You see, Larry, I've insured the necklace for nine months. For that period I've managed to get a special rate, but it's still a hell of a premium. If it's not sold within nine months, I'll have to pay more and I don't want to do that.'

I stood still, transfixed.

'You've insured it?'

'But of course, sweetie. You didn't imagine I would let you go all the way to Hong Kong with this necklace without insuring it? Anything could happen to you. Someone might even steal it from you. There could be an accident—God forbid! Three quarters of a million is a hell of a lot of money to risk.'

'Yes.' My heart was thumping now. 'Who did you insure it with?'

'Our people ... the National Fidelity. I had a terrible fight with that dreadful man Maddox! I hate him! He's so materialistic! Finally I had to go to one of the directors to get a cut rate. Maddox wanted to charge me nearly double.'

Maddox!

I too had had dealings with this man and I knew him to be the toughest, hardest and shrewdest claims assessor in the business: a man who smelt a crime before it was even thought of. He and his aide, Steve Harmas, had solved more insurance swindles and had jailed more people attempting to defraud than all the other insurance assessors put together.

Knowing I had lost colour, I turned away and walked slowly to the uncurtained picture window.

My mind was stiff with panic. The robbery was off! I had to stop it! But how? My brain just wouldn't work, but I did know it would be fatal to go ahead now Maddox was looming in the background.

Smart as the Paradise City police were, they were not in the same class as Maddox. I remembered a case* when Chief of Police Terrell was glad to co-operate with Maddox's investigator, Steve Harmas, and it was Harmas who had solved the theft of the Esmaldi necklace and also a murder.

'What's wrong, Larry?'

'Getting a headache, damn it!' I held my head in my hands while I tried to think what to do. Then I realised how absurdly easy it was to stop the robbery. I had only to cross the room, go out into the lobby, slip down the catch on the Yale lock and Rhea and Fel couldn't get in.

What could they do? What could they do except go away and curse me when we met again.

'I'll get you an Aspro,' Sydney said getting to his feet. 'Nothing like an Aspro, precious.'

'It's all right.' I started towards the door. 'I'll get it. They're in the bathroom cabinet, aren't they?'

'Let me...'

Then the door burst open and I knew I had left it too late.

Days later and looking back on that night, I was able to understand why the operation had blown up in my face.

The fault was entirely mine. In spite of my hours of thinking and careful planning, I had completely misjudged how

* See 'An Ear To the Ground.'

128

Sydney would react under pressure. I had been so certain that this willowy queer, with his buzzing and fluttering, wouldn't have the courage of a mouse and would shrivel with terror at any threat of violence. Had I not misjudged his courage, I wouldn't be in the position I now find myself, but I was sure he would present no problem and I never gave this vital part of the operation a thought.

I was moving towards the door and Sydney was coming around his desk when the door bust open and Fel, with Rhea behind him, came charging in.

Fel had on the Beatle wig and the silver glasses, an ugly looking Colt automatic in his fist. Behind him, her red hair concealed by a black scarf, her face hidden behind enormous silver goggles, Rhea also made a threatening sight, a .38 automatic in her gloved hand.

'Stay still!' Fel yelled: his voice spine chilling. 'Get your hands up!'

I was moving towards him. I tried to stop myself, but my legs kept moving. I was almost within reach of him when he swung at me. I saw the movement and tried to duck but the gun barrel smashed against my face and a white light exploded inside my skull. I felt warm blood running into my mouth and I was flat on my back, dazed by the violence of the blow. I lay there, my right eye rapidly closing, but my left eye registering what went on.

I saw Sydney grab hold of the Borgia dagger he used as a letter opener: an antique which had cost him thousands of dollars and of which he was very proud. He went for Fel like a charging bull, the gleaming dagger thrust forward, his face the colour of old parchment, his eyes bolting out of his head. He not only looked berserk but homicidal.

I saw Rhea back away and lift her gun, her lips coming off her teeth in a vicious snarl. There was a flash and a bang as Sydney stabbed at Fel who was standing motionless as if stupefied. The point of the dagger cut into Fels arm and blood spurted. The back of Sydney's head exploded into a red mushroom and he went down with a thud that shook the room.

Gunsmoke curled up to the ceiling. Fel staggered back,

holding his arm. Somehow with pain raging in my face, I got on to my hands and knees.

I stared at Sydney's body. Something horrible, white with blood, began oozing from the back of his head. He had to be dead. This I knew. Sydney! Dead! Something came loose in my mouth. I spat out a tooth on Sydney's two hundred year old Persian carpet. I started to crawl towards him. I wanted to touch him, to try to bring him back to life, then as I nearly reached him, I saw Rhea's shadow fall in front of me.

I stayed still, on my hands and knees, blood dripping from my mouth and I looked up. Opposite me was a big mirror. I saw her reflection in the mirror. The huge silver goggles, her white teeth, her lips drawn back in a vicious snarl, the blood-red trouser suit made her look like a demon escaped from hell.

She was holding the gun by its barrel. Even as I stared at her reflection, she set herself and smashed the gun butt down on my head.

When consciousness returned to me, I wasn't to know I had been in a coma for five days, had undergone brain surgery and twice had been given up as dead.

The first intimation of life I had as I seemed to swim upwards through murky water was the sound of a voice talking. I kept swimming higher and higher with no choking sensation, only a lazy, unwilling motion to reach the surface and I tuned into the voice speaking quite close to me and the words of the speaker penetrated.

He was saying, 'Look, Doc, how long do you think I've got to stick around here, waiting for this guy to come to? I'm losing out, sitting here. I'm the top man on the force. For God's sake, I've been sitting around here for five goddamn days!'

Force? The police?

Five days?

I lay motionless, now aware of a throbbing headache.

Another voice said, 'He could come out of this coma any moment. He could stay this way for months.'

'Months?' The other man's voice shot up. 'Isn't there any-thing you can do ... like giving him a shot or something? If I go on sitting here for months I'll go into a coma and then you'll have two patients in your lap.'

'I'm sorry ... we have to wait.'

'That's wonderful ... so what do I do ... practice Yoga?'

'That might be an idea, Mr. Lepski. Yoga is often very beneficial.'

There was a pause, then the man called Lepski, said, 'So you can't get him out of this goddamn coma?'

'No.'

'And it could be months?'

'Yes.'

'Boy! Do I pick them! Okay, Doc, so I sit.'

'It would seem so.'

Then the sound of footsteps crossing the room, a door opened and shut and the man called Lepski snorted, got to his feet and began to move around. His fidgeting became a back-ground sound. I was able to consider what had been said. I wished my head didn't ache so badly and wished I could think more clearly. With an effort of will, I forced my mind to look back into the past. I saw again that awful moment when Rhea had murdered Sydney. I saw her raise the gun, saw the flash, heard the bang again and saw poor, brave Sydney's head ex-plode in a mess of blood and brains.

I had been so stupid! Why had I misjudged his courage? I could see him charging at Fel, the Borgia dagger in his hand ... something I knew I could never have done in the face of a threatening gun. It had been a mad, reckless, but magnificent thing to have done, but only someone who had guts and real courage could have done it. Sydney must have known as soon as they had burst into the room, that they were after the neck-lace, but he didn't know the necklace he was trying to protect was of glass and he had given his life for nothing.

Well, he was dead. Now I was in the worst kind of trouble with a police officer sitting by my bedside waiting for me to talk. Did they suspect that I was involved in some way with the murder and the robbery? Surely that was unlikely? How was Maddox reacting, knowing that his company would have to pay out three-quarters of a million dollars? Knowing him, rather than pay out that enormous sum, he would dig and dig and dig until he came up with something that would hook me with the murder.

Well, I had time. If I remained still, gave no sign that I was now conscious, I might think of some way out . . . some way to save myself.

I heard the door open. A woman's voice said, 'Your lunch is ready, Mr. Lepski. I'll watch him.'

'Okay, baby. If he even lifts an eyelid call me. What's for lunch?'

'Beef stew.'

'Sure it's beef and not dog?'

She giggled.

'The Matron's cat has gone missing.'

'That's it! Boy! Do I get the breaks!' Then the door closed.

I heard the nurse sit down, then the pages of a book began to turn. I went back to my thoughts.

Rhea and Fel had taken the glass necklace. Fel had been wounded. Had the sound of the shot alerted anyone in the building? Had anyone seen them leaving? Maybe the police had them already and Rhea had talked. Maybe that was why this police officer was guarding me. I was sure if Rhea was caught, she would implicate me. But how to find out? I was also sure by the brief glimpse I had had of her expression in the mirror that she had meant to kill me as she had killed Sydney. But if I survived . . . as I seemed to be surviving . . . and if she and Fel were caught, then she would talk.

I wanted to lift my hands and press them to my aching head but I resisted the urge. I wanted time. I had to appear to be still in a coma.

Supposing she and Fel got away? What would they do? They had stolen a necklace they imagined to be worth at least a million dollars. They knew one false move would be disastrous. Would they try to sell the necklace? I had already warned them that no small fence would touch it. Now, with a

murder rap hanging over them, would they be so reckless as to approach any fence? Yet I could imagine Rhea with her inborn greed for money might not be able to resist the temptation of trying to turn the necklace into money.

But why think of them? If I was going to survive, I now had to think of myself.

Suppose the police or Maddox—especially Maddox—suspected I was behind the steal? Suppose they got a warrant and opened my safe? How would they react when they found the real necklace?

Then I saw a glimmer of hope ... a solution and dear God! how I needed a solution!

I lay still, my aching mind busy and it finally seemed to me that I could save myself ... always providing that the police never caught up with Rhea and Fel. If they didn't, then I was safe. I could muzzle Maddox. I could return to the showroom. With Sydney dead, Tom Luce would offer me a partnership. Without my expertise the shop could even fail. I suddenly felt lighter, relaxed and hopeful.

It could work out, but always providing Rhea and Fel were never caught.

But how could they be? No one, even if they had been seen leaving the apartment block could identify them. So long as they didn't do anything stupid like trying to sell the necklace, then surely they, as well as myself, were safe?'

But Rhea?

I remembered what Jenny had said: *She has this obsession about getting rich. She just won't accept the fact that if one wants money one has to work for it ... she says she won't wait that long.*

But Rhea was no one's fool. She must realise in spite of the temptation to make quick money the moment she tried to sell the necklace she was sunk.

Then I heard a tap on the door and the nurse get up and cross the room.

'Hello, Miss Baxter,' she said.

'How is he?' Jenny asked.

'Just the same.'

Jenny here!

It needed a great effort of will not to open my eyes. It was too soon for that. When I let them know I was conscious, I would have to do it slowly so that if this police officer turned tough I could retreat back into a faked coma. The knowledge that Jenny had come to Paradise City and was inquiring about me was like a shot in the arm to me.

'Could I see him?'

'Of course.'

I lay there, my heart pounding, as I heard movements by my bed.

'He looks so bad.' The distress in Jenny's voice meant a lot to me.

'That's to be expected. He's had brain surgery and it's been touch and go, but Dr. Summers says he is now out of danger. We just have to wait for him to come out of the coma.'

Cool fingers touched my wrist ... Jenny's fingers. I longed to open my eyes to look at her, to see her untidy hair and the expression of anxiety in her kind eyes, but it was too soon. For my own safety, I had to wait.

Then the sound of the door opening and another voice— Lepski's voice—broke in.

'If that was the Matron's cat, then I dig a cat lunch.' Lepski was back again. 'Hi, Miss Baxter,' he went on. 'You see he's still at it.'

'Yes.' I heard Jenny sigh. 'You will let me know the moment he comes to, nurse?'

'Of course.'

There were movements. I didn't dare look even between my eyelashes as I heard Lepski sit on a chair near me.

Then the door closed ... Jenny had gone.

'I like her,' Lepski said. 'She's got something. She loves this guy like crazy, doesn't she?'

'You can say that again,' the nurse said.

'Yeah.' There was a long pause, then Lepski went on, 'A couple of months ago I got promoted to Detective 1st Grade. You wouldn't believe it the way I get pushed around. Just sitting in this goddamn room day after day! They're trying to

kid me it's important.'

'I just can't follow what this is all about,' the nurse said. 'I wish you would explain it to me. I've read all the papers but they don't say a thing except Mr. Fremlin was murdered. Just what's going on?'

'Strictly between you and me, we don't know what's cooking either. Everything depends on Carr coming to the surface and telling us just what did happen. We think something important has been stolen, but we don't know what. So you don't understand what it's all about ... so that makes two of us.'

I was now listening intently.

'But surely you have some clues?' the nurse said.

'Baby, you have been reading too many detective stories.' Lepski's voice sounded bitter. 'All we know is a man and a woman broke into Fremlin's place, shot him, put Carr out of action and scrammed. We have a description of them. The nightman heard the shot and saw them leaving. His description amounts to nothing. So it depends on what Carr saw and what he knows. So I sit here. You get the photo?'

'I'm glad I'm not you.'

'That makes two of us.' A long pause, then Lepski asked, 'What's for supper?'

'You've just had your lunch, Mr. Lepski.'

'Never mind. I'm a man who looks ahead. What's for supper?'

'I wouldn't know. It depends on how the cook feels.'

'Is that right? How about telling her I'll give her a feel if she cooks up something good?'

The nurse giggled.

'That's not a nice way to talk, Mr. Lepski.'

'You're right. Sitting around here, looking at this guy turns me off. You going?'

'I certainly am before you get a feeling for me.'

'An idea! If I wasn't a respectably married man...'

I heard the sound of the door closing.

So they didn't know the necklace had been stolen. So Lawson had seen Rhea and Fel leave, but as Lepski had said, that didn't mean a thing. In their disguise and moving fast, they would be as good as anonymous. I lay still, thinking, then decided I mustn't come to the surface for at least a couple of hours. I mustn't let Lepski have an inkling that I had heard what he had told the nurse.

So I lay still and thought while time moved on. My head ached and Lepski's fidgeting irritated me. From time to time the nurse looked in. Finally, the doctor arrived and I decided now I could show signs of life. As I heard him greet Lepski, I moved, groaned softly, opened my eyes and looked up at a fat face bending over me, then I shut my eyes.

'He's coming to.'

'Man! Is that news!' Lepski exclaimed.

I opened my eyes again and raised my hand to my aching head and felt bandages.

'How do you feel, Mr. Carr?' This from the doctor.

'Where am I?' The classical remark made by people returning to consciousness.

'There's nothing for you to worry about. You're in the city hospital. How do you feel?'

'I have a headache.'

'I'll fix that. Don't worry. Just relax, Mr. Carr.'

'Sydney ... they killed him ...'

'Don't worry about a thing. I'll give you a shot and you take it easy. There's plenty of time ...'

'Hey! Hold it! I want to talk to him!' Lepski said, feverishly. 'This is important.'

'You don't talk to my patient yet.' There was a snap in the doctor's voice. 'Nurse ...'

A moment later I felt her dab my arm and then the prick of a needle. As I drifted off I thought that time was on my side. I was in no rush to talk to Lepski, but I knew in this coming game of poker, I held the better cards.

Sunlight woke me. I moved, raised my head, then blinked around. The pain in my head had gone. My mind was clear. Across the room, standing by the window was a tall, lean man with a heavy sun tan who I guessed was Lepski. Seated by my side was an attractive nurse who, seeing me move, got to her feet and bent over me.

'Hello, Mr. Carr ... feeling better now?'

'I'm feeling pretty good.' I lifted my hand to my head. 'What's been going on?'

'Just relax. I'll call Dr. Summers.'

She crossed the room to the telephone as Lepski converged on me. I found myself looking up into two hard pale blue eyes: cop's eyes.

'Hi, Mr. Carr,' he said, keeping his voice down. 'Am I glad to see you alive again. Do you feel like talking?'

'Who are you ... the doctor?'

Then Lepski was shoved aside by the nurse.

'Not yet,' she said to him. 'You don't talk to him without Dr. Summers' say-so.'

'Is this a goddamn ball!' Lepski said and walked back to the window.

A moment later a short fat man wearing a white coat came bustling in. He took my pulse, beamed at me, said I was doing fine and not to worry about anything.

'Mr. Carr, there's a police officer who wants to question you. Do you feel like talking to him? Don't hesitate to say no if you don't feel well enough, but it seems important.'

'It's about Sydney Fremlin?' I made my voice husky, a whisper.

'Yes.'

I closed my eyes and remained silent for several seconds. I wanted him to know I still felt pretty bad.

'All right.'

The doctor turned and beckoned to Lepski.

'Just a few minutes.'

Lepski came and stood by my side.

'Mr. Carr ... I can guess how you're feeling, but this is important. Can you tell me what happened? Just briefly ... just tell me what happened to have gotten you in this mess.'

I noted his voice wasn't hostile and that surely meant he wasn't suspicious of me.

Sounding weary and speaking in a whisper, I said, 'Fremlin and I were working. The door burst open. A man and a woman rushed in. Fremlin tried to stop them. The woman shot him and then she hit me.'

'What were you working on?'

'A design for a diamond collar.'

'Have you any idea what they were after?'

'The diamond necklace.'

'What necklace?'

'We were converting the necklace into a collar. The necklace was lying on the desk ... did they take it?'

'There was no necklace when we arrived,' Lepski said, leaning forward and staring at me. 'What necklace ... what was it worth?'

That would be enough for now, I told myself and wearily closed my eyes.

'That'll do,' Dr. Summers said. 'He must rest now.'

Lepski made a noise like a trapped bluebottle fly.

'This is a murder case, Doc. I've got to talk to him. Hey! Mr. Carr!'

I opened my eyes, stared at him, then closed my eyes. I got another prick in the arm and I drifted away, hearing Lepski protesting.

When I came to again, I found another man sitting by my side. He was tall, lean and ugly in a pleasant way with an easy quiet manner.

'How are you, Mr. Carr?'

Behind him hovered the nurse.

'A bit doped,' I said, shut my eyes, moved my head, then looked at him again. 'Who are you?'

'I'm Steve Harmas,' he told me. 'I represent the National Fidelity Insurance Corporation.'

I felt a cold chill start up my spine.

So this was the man who I had heard so much about: the man who solved frauds and murders with Maddox behind him.

This man would be far more dangerous than Lepski. I was sure of that, but I couldn't stall any longer. This was the showdown. I had to convince him or I was sunk.

'Feel like talking?' Harmas asked. His voice was quiet and he had this bedside manner, but I wasn't conned.

'Yes.' I made out I was making an effort and I raised myself slightly so I could look directly at him. 'Go ahead.'

'I'll make it brief, Mr. Carr.' His voice wasn't hostile, but his eyes were watchful. He didn't con me for a moment. 'Did you know Mr. Fremlin had insured a diamond necklace for three-quarters of a million dollars?'

'Yes ... he told me.'

'We get the idea the necklace has been stolen. From what you told Lepski, it was the necklace they were after. Mr. Fremlin's safe was open ... no sign of the necklace. Did they get it?'

'No.'

He stared at me.

'They didn't? Are you sure?'

'Yes.'

He regarded me doubtfully.

'Do you know where it is?'

Here it is, I thought, now I play my ace card.

'Yes, I know ... it's in my safe in my apartment.'

There was a long pause as Harmas regarded me, his eyes quizzing.

'In your safe, Mr. Carr? I'm not following you.'

I closed my eyes and pretended to rest, then looking at him again, I said, 'I can assure you the necklace hasn't been stolen. There were two necklaces. The original in diamonds and an imitation in glass. We were working with the imitation.'

Harmas let breath whistle out between his teeth.

'Is that good news! My boss thought we were going to be stuck for a three-quarters of a million claim! You really mean this?'

'Yes. Fremlin was scared to have the real necklace in his apartment. He asked me to house it in my safe. Unless the thieves have been to my apartment, then the necklace is still in my safe.'

'Could I check, Mr. Carr? My boss is having one coronary after the other and I'd like to put him out of his misery.'

'Go ahead. You'll find my apartment key in my jacket pocket.' I gave him the address. 'The combination of the safe is X-11-0-4. Go ahead,' and I closed my eyes.

'You take it easy, Mr. Carr. Don't worry about a thing,' and he was gone.

I drew in a long deep breath. Surely, I thought, this has got me off the hook. But there was this risk: if the police caught up with Rhea and Fel, they would talk, then this slick inspiration of mine would come unstuck at the seams.

EIGHT

Sergeant Fred Hess, in charge of the Homicide squad, was a short, fat man with bushy eyebrows, cold eyes and a quizzing, alert manner.

An hour after Harmas had gone, Hess, followed by Lepski, entered my room and converged on me.

'Mr. Carr ... I'm Hess: City Police, Homicide,' he said in a voice that sounded like a fall of gravel. 'Dr. Summers says you aren't fit enough to make a full statement, but I'm hoping you feel like answering a few questions.'

'I'm all right,' I said. 'Dr. Summers means well, but he fusses.'

This went down well with Hess who gave a little grin, pulled up a chair and sat by my bedside. Lepski went over to the window, sat down and took out a notebook.

I had had plenty of time to go over my story and I was ready and fairly confident.

'Okay, Mr. Carr, suppose you tell me about this necklace. Harmas tells me the killers stole an imitation. Is that right?'

'If the necklace is missing, then they stole the imitation.'

'Would they know it was a fake?'

'No, it would fool anyone but a top expert. But to get this straight, Sergeant, suppose I give you the story right from the start.'

He squinted at me, then nodded.

'That would be fine.'

So I told him how Mrs. Plessington had wanted a necklace, how I had a glass replica made so she would be able to make up her mind if the design was what she wanted. I explained

141

after the sale, Sydney had wanted to sell the imitation but that, since it had been my biggest sale, I had decided to keep it as a souvenir. I said Sydney went along with this (My first lie.) and that I had paid him three thousand dollars for the necklace. Then I went on to tell Hess about Mrs. P.'s gambling urge and how, in panic to cover her losses, she had asked Sydney to sell the necklace. I explained why the deal had to be in secret and how Sydney and I got the idea of converting the necklace into a collar. I went on to explain that Sydney had decided, to prevent any leak, to work on the collar in his apartment.

'But Sydney was scared to have the necklace in his apartment and I suggested we used the imitation to work with,' I went on. 'Then he asked me to spread the risk by keeping the original necklace in my safe.'

'Just a moment, Mr. Carr,' Hess broke in. So far, he had sat still, his face expressionless, listening. 'I'd like to get this clear. We've examined both your safe and Mr. Fremlin's safe. Fremlin's safe is a better one than yours. His safe is wired to police headquarters: yours isn't. How come Fremlin thought it safer for you to keep the necklace?'

This was a question I expected him to ask and I had the answer ready.

'Sydney was nervous,' I said. 'He thought it unlikely any thief would suspect I had anything worthwhile in my safe whereas he felt he could be the focus for thieves.'

'Yeah.' Hess scratched his nose. 'Nervous, huh? You mean he was nervous someone would break in?'

'He had paid for this necklace out of his own money. Although he had insured it, he wanted to divide the risks.'

'That's not the question, Mr. Carr. He was nervous?'

'Yes.'

'Then how come he never locked his front door?'

'He was always forgetting his keys. His manservant will tell you the same. He felt secure, leaving his front door unlocked because he knew the entrance door downstairs was always kept locked.'

'Yet it wasn't locked on the night of the robbery. How

come?'

'I wouldn't know. When I arrived just after 10 o'clock, the door was locked. I had to buzz for Lawson, the doorman, to let me in. Claude, Mr. Fremlin's manservant, was leaving and he and I had a brief talk, but Lawson returned to his office. Maybe he forgot to lock up after Claude had gone.'

'Lawson said he didn't lift the catch on the lock so when the door shut after Claude, it would lock automatically,' Hess said.

'It didn't, did it? Otherwise these two wouldn't have got in, would they?'

'Yeah.' Hess stared down at his fat, brown hands, his forehead in wrinkles. 'Lawson heard the shot and came out of his office as the killers came out of the elevator. They both had guns in their hands. Lawson is no hero. He stepped back out of sight, but he's given us a description of them.' He paused, then went on, 'When a man's scared, he's likely to be an unrealiable witness. I'd like you to give me a description of these two as you saw them, Mr. Carr.'

'Don't imagine I wasn't scared,' I said. 'It happened so suddenly. The door burst open and these two rushed in, yelling at us. I was going to the bathroom for an Aspro and walked right into them. The man hit me across the face and I went down.' I went on to describe how Sydney had gone for the man and how the woman had shot him, then as I was crawling towards Sydney, she had hit me.

'So it was the woman? She shot Fremlin and knocked you out?'

'Yes.'

'The man was wounded?'

'Sydney cut his arm with the dagger.'

'Yeah. We have this blood group from the dagger,' Hess said. He spoke casually but his words sent a sudden chill through me. A blood group! One small step towards pinning the murder on Fel if he was ever caught.

'Let's take the man first, Mr. Carr,' Hess went on. 'Will you give me a description of him as you saw him?'

'He was heavily built,' I said, 'about your height. (My

143

second lie.) He had on a Beatle wig, big silver lensed goggles and a red jacket with black patch pockets.' I put my hand wearily to my head. 'That's the best I can do.'

'Heavily built and about five foot eight?'

'Yes.'

Hess rubbed the tip of his nose.

'Lawson says he was tall: around six foot and thin.'

Confusion was my main hope.

'That wasn't my impression.'

'Yeah.' Hess sighed. 'In a set-up like this no witness ever seems to agree.' He shrugged. 'But the wig, goggles and jacket match. Now about the woman.'

'I didn't register her much except she had on big silver goggles which blotted out her face. I think she was big and powerfully built for a woman. She gave me the impression of being around forty-five: a mature woman. She had on red trousers and her hair hidden by a black scarf.'

The door opened and Dr. Summers came in.

'I think, Sergeant, that must be all for today,' he said firmly. 'I said twenty minutes.'

'Sure.' Hess got to his feet. 'Well, thanks, Mr. Carr. You take it easy. Thanks for your help. I'll be seeing you again.'

He and Lepski left the room.

Doctor Summers took my pulse, told me I should now have a nap and that my lunch would be coming in about an hour. When he had gone, I lay still and thought over what I had told Hess. It seemed to be going well except for the blood group. But there was nothing I could do about that. I knew my safety depended on whether Rhea and Fel were caught. But providing Rhea didn't try to sell the necklace, I couldn't see how they could be caught.

After lunch and after a nap, the nurse came in and told me Miss Baxter was asking to see me.

'Do you feel like another visitor, Mr. Carr,' she asked with a knowing smile.

I said I did.

Jenny came in with a bunch of red roses and a basket of hothouse grapes. She stood at the foot of my bed and regarded me

144

and there was a light in her eyes that really did things for me.

Her hair was neat and tidy. She had on a navy blue coat and shirt with a frilled white blouse and she looked marvellous to me.

'How do you feel, Larry?'

I grinned at her.

'We've changed places ... roses and grapes too. How's your ankle?'

'Coming along.' She moved awkwardly to the chair by my bedside and sat down. 'Tell me ... how do you feel?'

'I'm okay ... now you're here.' I held out my hand and she took it. 'Jenny ... this is marvellous. Thank you for coming. Where are you staying?'

'Oh ... a little hotel. When I read about it in the paper, I just had to come.'

'This is a hell of a thing,' I said. 'Sydney was my friend. I still can't believe he is dead.'

'You must try not to think about it. It doesn't do any good. The thing for you to do is to get well.'

'That's right. You remember when I called you ... the evening when it happened? I thought I was saying goodbye to you. Odd how things work out, isn't it?'

She nodded.

'The doctor said I mustn't tire you. I'm not going to stay any longer,' and she got to her feet.

'Hey! Wait a minute! You've only just arrived.'

'I wanted to see you. Is there anything I can bring you tomorrow?'

'Sit down, for God's sake! I want to talk to you. How long can you stay in Paradise City?'

'Two or three days.'

'Don't tell me with that ankle of yours you can start work yet, Jenny.'

'No ... I can't, but ...' She smiled. 'I can't afford to stay here. This must be the most expensive city in the world.'

'Yes, it certainly is.' I paused and looked at her. 'I don't know how long I'll have to stay here. It could be several weeks. Would you do me a favour?'

'Of course, Larry.'

'Check out of that hotel and move into my apartment.'

Her eyes opened wide.

'I couldn't do that!'

'This is a business proposition. I must have someone there to answer the telephone, look after my mail, keep the place in order. I have a coloured woman who comes in twice a week and if she isn't supervised she'll do nothing. There's a spare bedroom you can have and I pay a willing housekeeper a hundred dollars a week ... all found. That's the favour, Jenny. Please ...'

She hesitated, then as she began to shake her head, I went on, 'The favour also includes coming to see me every day so I won't feel neglected and lonely.'

She smiled.

'All right, Larry, but I'm not going to be paid. I have some money of my own. Honest ... I won't do it otherwise.'

My blonde nurse came in.

'It's time for Mr. Carr's nap, Miss Baxter,' she said, smiling at Jenny.

'Nurse, would you give Miss Baxter the key of my apartment, please?' I said. 'Mr. Harmas had it. I expect he has returned it by now.'

'Yes, he has.' The nurse looked at Jenny and then at me and gave me a sly little grin. 'Come with me, Miss Baxter.'

Jenny patted my hand.

'I'll be in tomorrow afternoon,' and she followed the nurse out of the room.

The following morning, soon after Dr. Summers had been in to see me, I had an unexpected visitor. I was feeling depressed because Summers had said I would have to stay in hospital for at least another two weeks. Even when I returned home I would have to be careful not to exert myself.

My unexpected visitor was Tom Luce. He came into my room looking more like a bulldog than ever, wearing a dark, immaculate suit, his balding head glistening with sweat beads.

I had seldom had much to do with him as I had always

146

worked with Sydney, but I knew him to be tough, loya
financial wizard.

'Well, Larry,' he said, sitting down by my side. 'I'm
to find you in this state. What a terrible thing! Poor Syc
His funeral was yesterday. A wonderful turn out ... ever
who is anyone was there. I had a wreath in your name p
the best place. You have never seen so many flowers.'

Inwardly, I winced and was thankful I hadn't been there.

'Thanks, Tom. It's a hell of a thing. I still can't believe h
gone.'

'No.' Luce shook his head. 'I've been talking to Dr. Sur
mers. From what he tells me, Larry, you'll be out of action fo
three or four months. Can you suggest anyone we can get t
take your place until you can get back?'

I had been thinking of this problem.

'You'll need a designer and an assistant to work with Terry.
I know Hans Kloch wants a change. He's a good designer: not
quite in Sydney's class, but good enough. Why not write to
him? He's with Werner of Antwerp. Then there's Pierre Martin. He's with Cartiers, Los Angeles. I think he would jump at
the chance.'

Luce made notes on the back of an envelope.

'I'll get on to them right away. Terry and Miss Barlow are
really stretched.' Again he paused, then said, 'You should
know right away, Larry, that you are now the senior partner.'

'Senior partner?' I stared at him. 'You mean you are offering me a partnership, Tom?'

'Of course I would have offered you a partnership, but Sydney has willed you all his holdings, so that makes you senior
partner without my say-so. I am most happy about this, Larry.
I wouldn't want a better man to work with.'

I felt a rush of cold blood up my spine.

'Tom! What are you saying? I don't understand.'

'I've read his will. There are a few bequests, but the bulk of
his estate which is considerable goes to you.'

'To me?' My voice shot up.

'Yes. I've brought along a copy of the will and a list of his
assets. As you probably know I handle all his affairs. Sydney

as very fond of you, Larry. As he says in his will you will make a worthy successor and I agree with that.'

I couldn't help it. I was still weak and I had little or no control over myself. I began to weep, hiding my face in my hands while violent sobs shook me. How I hated myself! I had been directly responsible for Sydney's death! If I hadn't planned to rob him of the necklace, he would be alive today. And in return for my treachery, he had left me the bulk of his estate.

The nurse came in, took one look at me, waved Luce out of the room and called Dr. Summers.

The next thing I knew was feeling a prick in my arm and I drifted off into blessed oblivion.

I was under sedation for the rest of the day. When Dr. Summers came to see me the following morning, he said I was not to have any visitors for the next three days. This emotional upset of mine must not be repeated.

In a way I was glad, although I was going to miss Jenny's visits, but it did give me time to think about my future.

I read Sydney's will. He had left his fine collection of Wedgwood and Spode to Luce. Claude received a hundred thousand dollars. His secretary and Miss Barlow had ten thousand each. Terry had Sydney's personal jewellery. The rest of his estate came to me.

Luce had listed Sydney's assets. His stock holdings were worth a million and a half. There was the penthouse and a number of valuable paintings, including the Picasso. There was his Rolls Corniche and the contents of the penthouse and I knew that included Mrs. P.'s necklace.

I read through the list and I was dazzled, then I told myself I couldn't possibly accept all this. I could never live with myself if I did. I thought like that for several hours, then it occurred to me it would not only be difficult but also dangerous to refuse. After more thought I began to persuade myself that I wasn't responsible for Sydney's death. Hadn't I told Fel not to load the guns? How was I to know that Rhea was so vicious she wouldn't hesitate to kill? How could I possibly

know? Hadn't I suffered also? It was pure chance that I too hadn't been killed. I was sure Rhea had meant to kill me. Hadn't I warned Fel not to hit me over the head and hadn't she been there when I had warned him?

At the end of two days of constant thought, I began to realize what Sydney's money and possessions would mean to me. I would be a rich man. I would be senior partner of the best and oldest established jewellers in the city. If I wanted to I could move into his penthouse. Why not? I would make a few changes, but it was one of the finest penthouses in the city and I had often wished it were mine.

I would even ask Claude if he would continue to run the place. I had no idea what Sydney paid him, but if he could afford Claude, then with his money, so could I.

Then my thinking shifted to Jenny. Did I want to marry her? Did she want to marry me? We had known each other for only a short time but I had this thing for her and surely she wouldn't have come to Paradise City to be with me if she, in her turn, hadn't a thing for me.

The doctor had told me that as soon as I left hospital I should go on a long cruise. This seemed to be the solution. I would ask Jenny to come with me and we would be able to get to know each other during the two months on the ship. This idea excited me. When Dr. Summers came around in the evening, he said I was making excellent progress.

'Could I see Miss Baxter tomorrow?' I asked.

'Of course. I'll get nurse to telephone her.'

When the nurse brought my supper, I asked her to let me have the newspapers. I felt it was time to know what was being said about Sydney, the murder and myself.

After a little delay—I guessed she was consulting Dr. Summers—she turned up with copies of *The Paradise Herald* for the past five days.

'We haven't bothered you with your mail, Mr. Carr,' she told me, 'but there are two sacks of letters from well wishers. Miss Baxter is checking them at your apartment.'

I said that was fine with me and settled down to read the papers.

The report of what happened at Sydney's apartment on that fatal night stated that while Sydney and I were working on designs for a diamond collar, a man and a woman had burst into the apartment, guns in hand. The reporter said that I had tried to close with them, but received a stunning blow across my face, knocking me half unconscious and that Sydney, attacking the man with a paper knife, had been shot to death by the woman.

The two bandits had immediately fled before the alarm could be raised. They had been seen leaving by the doorman and the reporter went on to give a detailed description of them. He added that the police would make no comment as to whether the bandits had stolen anything. This puzzled me as it seemed to puzzle the reporter. Why no mention of the necklace?

Turning to yesterday's *Herald*, its headline came as a blow in the face to me.

DIAMOND EXPERT INHERITS THE FREMLIN MILLIONS

My photograph accompanied the report which stated that I had worked for Fremlin for the past five years. I was considered one of the leading diamond experts and that Fremlin had left the bulk of his vast fortune to me and I was now Luce & Fremlin's senior partner. The reporter had raked up my engagement (how long ago that seemed now), told how Judy had died, explained how I had gone to Luceville on the advice of the famous alienist, Dr. Melish, for a change of scene, how I had worked with the poor, had returned to Paradise City and now because of Fremlin's death was his successor and a millionaire.

I read and re-read this report feeling as cold as a dead man. Would the Morgans see it? If they did what would they do? For several minutes I felt sick with an awful nagging fear, then I got control of myself.

What could they do? I asked myself. If they gave me away, they would give themselves away. It would be their word against mine. Rhea was no fool. She must realise that to give me away would be suicidal.

But suppose the police caught them? That was the danger. If they were caught, then they would talk. How would I stand then?

I thought about this. With Sydney's money behind me to buy the best legal brains, the fact that I had made no mystery about where the real necklace was and if I denied everything they said, surely no jury would convict me.

Well, they weren't caught. Maybe they had already left the country. They had over a thousand dollars of mine: enough for them to get to Mexico and go into hiding.

I was glad when the nurse came in with a sleeping pill and settled me for the night.

Around 1000, Jenny came into my room with more red roses. She said she loved my apartment, was getting on fine with Cissy, my coloured help, was coping with my enormous mail and thought I looked better.

'I'm fine,' I said. 'Now listen, Jenny, you've seen the *Herald*? You know Sydney has left me all his money?'

She nodded.

'It's wonderful for you, Larry, but I can understand how you feel about it.'

We looked at each other.

'At first I thought of refusing it, but then I realised refusing all this money wouldn't bring Sydney back to life.'

'You couldn't refuse ... he wanted you to have it.'

'Yes.' Then I went on to tell her Dr. Summers had recommended a two month sea voyage. He had suggested I should take a companion with me so I shouldn't have to exert myself. I looked at her. 'Would you like to come, Jenny? It would mean organising everything and it would entail quite a bit of work, but I'd much rather have you with me than anyone else.'

She stared at me as if she didn't believe what I was saying.

'It would be quite a trip,' I went on. 'South Africa, India, Ceylon, Hong Kong and Australia. What do you say?'

'You really mean it?'

'Of course I mean it.'

151

'Oh, Larry ... I would love it!' She was so excited she clapped her hands and I remembered how excited she had been when I had taken her to dinner at Luceville.

'You'll have to get busy. I should be ready to leave in about four weeks. Buy yourself all the clothes you want and don't forget I'm very rich. Charge everything to my bank. See Tom Luce. He'll fix credit for you. Go to the Outward Bound ... they are my travel agents. Get them to prepare a schedule and we'll go through it together. First class, of course: a stateroom and a single cabin for you. Will you do that?'

'I'll see Mr. Luce and the travel agents this afternoon.'

After more talk, her face flushed, her eyes sparkling, Jenny left me.

I relaxed back on my pillow and for the first time since I had been in this hospital I felt reasonably safe and reasonably happy ... but not for long.

In the afternoon Sergeant Hess and Lepski visited me.

'Just a question or two, Mr. Carr, if you feel like it,' Hess said, sitting by my bedside.

I braced myself. What was coming?

'There's a question I want to ask you, sergeant,' I said. 'I've been reading the papers. There's no mention of the Plessington necklace ... any reason?'

'Sure ... if we gave out the necklace had been stolen, Mr. Carr,' Hess said, 'we would have to say it was a fake. So long as the thieves imagine they have a genuine necklace they will try to sell it. We have alerted every big fence in the country. If they try to sell it we'll have them.'

'I see.'

I thought of Rhea's greed. Would she be reckless enough to take such a risk?

Hess shifted in his chair.

'I understand, Mr. Carr, you did welfare work for a few weeks in Luceville. Is that correct?'

I regarded him, my heart beginning to thump.

'Yes. It's in the papers, Sergeant, there's no mystery about it. Dr. Melish advised me to have a change of scene after my accident and sent me to work with his niece, Miss Baxter.

152

Why do you ask?'

'Does the name Rhea Morgan mean anything to you?'

Somehow I met his steady stare. Somehow I managed to keep my face expressionless.

'Yes . . . Miss Baxter will tell you more about her than I can.'

'You had something to do with this woman?'

'Yes. When Miss Baxter was in hospital, I volunteered to meet Rhea Morgan when she was released from prison and drive her home . . . you could call it a welfare service.'

'Did she know who you are?'

'She knew my name.'

'Did she know you were working for Luce & Fremlin . . . did you mention that to her?'

'No. I didn't like the woman. We scarcely said anything to each other.'

'But she could have found out who you were?'

'I suppose so. But why should she?'

'I'm trying to fill in blank spaces, Mr. Carr.'

'Has Rhea Morgan anything to do with this—this investigation?' I was now aware my hands had turned moist.

'We're beginning to think so. The Luceville police received information from an attendant working at the Caltex gas station, just outside Luceville. He had seen the reports in the papers giving a description of the two killers. He called up Sergeant O'Halloran of the city police and told him that the previous week he had been held up by a man wearing a Beatle wig, silver goggles and a red jacket with black patch pockets. This man had a toy gun and was nervous. The attendant told him to scram which he did. The attendant thought no more about it until he read in the papers that a man answering the description of this hold-up phoney was wanted for murder. O'Halloran called me and I went up to Luceville. This seemed to me, Mr. Carr, an odd, coincidence. Here was a man matching the description of the killer in Luceville and you had been in Luceville. So O'Halloran and I looked around for someone with a record who had contacted you. This was a long shot, but police work is mostly long shots, and we came up with

Rhea Morgan. It didn't look such a long shot when we found out she lived with her brother. Have you met her brother?'

I had to moisten my lips before saying, 'Yes. He was there when I brought her home.'

'At no time, Mr. Carr, did you mention you were in the diamond trade to these two?'

'I'm sure of that.'

Hess brooded for a moment.

'You had a car?'

'Yes.'

'If they wanted to know more about you, they could have checked your licence, couldn't they?'

'But why should they? After all, I was just a welfare worker to them, bringing the woman home.'

'Yeah.' He paused, then asked, 'Could these two have been the two who killed Fremlin?'

I paused as if thinking, then I said, 'I don't know. It happened so quickly. I couldn't possibly say.'

'Would you say Morgan was the same build at the man who burst into the apartment?'

'I don't think so ... I told you ... I—I was under the impression the man was short and heavily built. Morgan is tall and thin.'

Hess nodded.

'Yeah.' He rubbed his ear, frowning. 'O'Halloran and I went to Morgan's place ... little better than a shack. We found the place shut up ... no one there. We asked around. The Morgans haven't been seen since two days before the murder. It would take them that time to drive down here. We've been checking all the hotels and motels and we've come up with something.' Again he stroked his nose. 'They stayed at the Pyramid Motel and checked out on the night of the killing. The clerk there identified Rhea's photo. Tell me something: you met and talked to her. Would you say she was a killer?'

I thought of Rhea's reflection in the glass she set herself to hit me. A killer? Yes ... she was a killer.

'I can't answer that, Sergeant,' I said, my voice husky.

'How could I possibly know?'

'Yeah ... but she has a hell of a record. I like these two for the job. If Morgan's got a wounded arm and if his blood group jells, I guess we've got them.' He got to his feet. 'There's an alarm out for them right now. It's only a matter of time before we pick them up.' He jerked his head at Lepski who made for the door. 'Okay, Mr. Carr, I don't think I'll have to worry you much longer. You take it easy.'

He followed Lepski out of the room.

I had dug my own grave, I told myself.

How could I have been so brainless and stupid to have given Fel that disguise, having used it myself on that spineless hold-up attempt? I had been so confident, warning them to use gloves and providing them with an alibi, but it had never occurred to me that the fat gas service attendant would hook them to Luceville because of the Beatle wig, the goggles and the jacket!

So within only a few days, when I had felt so sure they couldn't be identified unless they tried to sell the necklace, the police were on to them!

Now they were being hunted. How long would they survive? When they were caught, they would talk!

Radio Paradise put out a news broadcast every three hours. I became a compulsive listener. Every time the commentator said, 'and here is the news ...' I would stiffen, my heart would begin to thump while I waited to hear if they were caught.

During the three hour wait, I was scarcely civil to my nurse. I went off my food. I could only watch the hands of my watch crawling around to the next news broadcast.

I realised the two month sea trip must be cancelled. The idea of being on a ship, cut off from the news, wondering all the time if they had been caught, expecting to find detectives at any port waiting to arrest me would drive me crazy.

I found I was so restless. I couldn't remain in bed and the following morning as soon as the nurse had gone, I got up and began to pace the floor, feeling unsteady at first, but as I persisted, stronger for the exercise.

Dr. Summers found me standing by the window.

'Now don't fuss,' I said. 'I want to go home. I don't give a damn if it's good for me or bad for me. If I take it easy on my terrace in the sun, I know I'll make good progress and I can't stand being cooped up here any longer!'

Rather to my surprise, he agreed.

'All right, Mr. Carr, I'll order an ambulance and you can go home this afternoon. I'll drop in this evening to see how you are getting on. I think it would be wise for Nurse Flemming to go along with you and stay with you for a few days ... just in case.'

'I don't want her. Miss Baxter can take care of me.'

By 1600 that afternoon I was back in my apartment, sitting in the sun on the terrace.

It was when Jenny arrived, carrying a tray of tea things that I told her the sea trip was off.

The shocked disappointment in her eyes irritated me. I kept looking at my watch. The radio news would be coming up in fifteen minutes.

'But why?' Jenny asked. 'It'll do you so much good. What has made you change your mind?'

'I can change my mind, can't I?' I snapped. 'I want to get back to work. I have to cope with Sydney's estate. I realise now to spend two months on a ship would bore me stiff.'

'Oh.' She looked down at her hands and she flushed. 'But I've ordered clothes, Larry. You said ...'

'That's all right. We might go later ... who knows? Keep them. You deserve them.'

'I can't do that, Larry. I was going to be your secretary ...'

'Don't bother me with that! Keep them!' Again I looked at my watch.

'Thank you.' There was a sudden cold note in her voice. After a long pause, she said, 'I think I should go back to Luceville. I'm walking quite well now. I think you can do without me, can't you?'

I suddenly knew I had to be alone. I had to spend my time waiting and listening to the news and Jenny would be in the way. Besides, if they were caught and when they talked, I didn't want Jenny to be here when I was arrested. That was something I didn't want.

Without looking at her, I said, 'All right, Jenny. I understand. You want to get back to your work as much as I want to get back to mine.'

'Yes.'

'All right ... that's settled. I ...' Seeing it was news time I broke off. 'Just a moment ... I want to hear the news.'

It was while I was listening to the same dreary rigmarole about Nixon and China, Vietnam, England and the Common Market that Jenny got quietly to her feet and went into the sitting-room.

When the rigmarole came to an end with no news of their arrest, I too went into the sitting-room. She wasn't there. I hesitated, then went to the spare bedroom. She was packing.

'You don't have to rush off like this,' I said uneasily. 'What are you thinking of?'

She went on packing.

'There's a bus in an hour. If I catch it, I'll be at my desk the day after tomorrow and I want that,' she said.

'Yes ... I see.'

Sick with myself, I went back to the terrace. Twenty minutes later she joined me.

'Look after yourself, Larry,' she said. 'Don't overdo things.'

'Thanks for being such a help. I'll keep in touch.' I couldn't look at her.

'There's something worrying you, isn't there?' she asked and put her hand on my arm. 'Won't you tell me? Two are often better than one when solving a problem.'

How I wanted to tell her!

But what was the use? What could she do? There wasn't anything anyone could do.

'It's all right, Jenny,' I said curtly. 'Don't miss your bus.'

She regarded me for a long moment, her lips trembling. I knew then she really loved me, but like everything I touched now ... it was too late.

I turned away. A moment later I heard the front door shut and then I knew I was really alone.

NINE

During the next three days I remained alone, sending down to the restaurant for meals and listening to every news broadcast.

The telephone gave me little peace: people inquiring after my health, my friends wanting to come and see me and sounding hurt when I said I wasn't well enough to see anyone. Finally, I gave up answering it.

On the third morning Dr. Summers removed my bandages. Apart from a bald patch at the back of my head, he told me I was as good as new. Now was the time, he went on, for me to take a sea trip. I said I was thinking about it and got rid of him.

I began to regret treating Jenny the way I had done. I had been in such a panic I just had had to be by myself, but now I was getting over my scare, I tried to assure myself that Rhea and Fel might never be caught. For all I knew they could be in Mexico or even South America while I could spend the rest of my days chained to the radio.

Should I call Jenny, explain that I had been upset and that now I felt I could face a sea trip? Would she forget my behaviour and come with me?

I hesitated.

Maybe, I thought, I'd better wait a couple of weeks, then if there was no news of the Morgans, I would go.

I wrote Jenny a letter, trying to explain how bad I had been feeling and that I was better now and if she would come with me, I wanted to make the sea trip before long, but after reading it, it seemed to me to be so insincere that I tore it up.

On the fourth day, I made the effort and took a taxi to the shop. In my briefcase I had the Plessington necklace.

I received a big welcome from Miss Barlow, Pierre Martin and Hans Kloch. Even Terry, although not enthusiastic, did have the grace to say he hoped I was better.

I went into Tom Luce's office and put the case containing the necklace on his desk.

'Tom ... I want to explain about the necklace,' I said.

He gave me a rather old-fashioned look, nodded and waited.

I told him the truth: how Sydney had wanted to make the re-sale of the necklace a private deal, how I had warned him this wasn't ethical and how he had persisted.

'I know that,' Luce said quietly. 'You see, Larry, not much escapes me. I handled Sydney's stocks and when he told me he wanted to sell a block worth three-quarters of a million and when I heard Mrs. P. was up to her eyes in debt, it wasn't hard to put two and two together. It didn't worry me and I'm sorry it worried Sydney.'

'The necklace is mine now,' I said. 'I'm handing it over to the firm, Tom. When we sell it, using Sydney's design, I want the firm to make the profit.'

'That's the way a partner should act,' he said, 'but the firm will buy it off you at what Sydney paid. That's fair enough, isn't it? The profit of the sale goes into the firm.'

'Fine ... buy me some stock, Tom. You looked after Sydney's affairs, I'd be grateful if you'll look after mine.'

That pleased him.

We talked about the business. Both Martin and Kloch were giving satisfaction and even Terry was behaving himself.

'I don't think you should start work yet, Larry,' Luce said. 'You don't look right. Why don't you take a sea trip?'

'I'm thinking about it, but not just yet. I'm going over to Sydney's penthouse now. Before I take a trip, I have to get rid of my apartment and the furniture and settle in the penthouse. So I'll be around for a week or so. If anything comes up that looks tricky, you can always consult me.'

Leaving him, I drove to Sydney's apartment block. Harry Gregson, the day porter, saluted me as I crossed to his desk.

'Glad to see you about again, Mr. Carr,' he said. 'A real nasty business. I miss Mr. Sydney ... he was a gentleman.'

'Yes.' A pause, then I went on, 'I'm taking over the penthouse, Harry. Have you the keys?'

'Yes, sir. I saw about it in the papers. I said then as I say now: good luck to you, Mr. Carr. The staff here are very pleased you will be living here.'

'Thank you, Harry.'

'No one's been up there since the police left it. It'll need cleaning before you move in.'

'Do you have Claude's address, Harry? I was wondering if he would work for me.'

'I don't see why not. Yeah, I've got his telephone number. Just a moment ...' He went into his office and after searching through a desk drawer he came out with a slip of paper. 'I heard he was pretty upset.'

'He hasn't been here since... ?'

'No, sir. He went to stay with his old mother for a couple of weeks, but I guess he could be back by now.'

'I'll call him.' Taking the slip of paper and the keys of the penthouse, I went on, 'Thanks, Harry. I'm just taking a quick look around. I won't be long.'

As the elevator took me up to the penthouse my thoughts went back to that fatal night. I flinched at the thought of entering Sydney's home for the first time since his death.

As I paused outside the front door, I hesitated. I had a feeling of sick uneasiness, but this was crazy, I told myself. Sydney was dead. This marvellous penthouse now belonged to me ... it was to be my future home! I must rid myself of this guilt complex. I was not responsible for his death! I had told myself that over and over again during my long hours of loneliness. I had to get this feeling of guilt out of my mind.

I sank the key into the lock and moved into the lobby. I could hear the faint whirring of the air conditioner and I paused, listening. Had the police left the air conditioner on? Hadn't anyone been up here to make sure the lights and the air conditioner had been turned off?

Puzzled, I pushed open the door.

Facing me, gun in hand, was Fel Morgan.

On the floor below came the sound of a dog yapping, then the murmur of voices, then the dog yapped again.

I stood motionless, staring at the gun that could produce death.

Faintly through the double glazing I could hear the siren of an ambulance. Far below and away from me, Paradise City was living its life.

I shifted my eyes from the gun to Fel's face. As I did so, he lowered the gun and said in a shuddering, terrified voice, 'Jesus God! I thought you were the fuzz!'

I saw then that he was more frightened than I was and this steadied me, although my heart was pounding and my mouth was dry. I stared at him.

What a god-awful wreck he looked!

He was dirty and emaciated; his face covered with red stubble. I could smell his dirt. He wore the red jacket with the black patch pockets but it was scarcely recognisable under its layer of filth. His shoes were mud encrusted as if he had been walking in a swamp. His eyes were sunken and frightened. His mouth twitched. His breath came in quick short gasps through his dirty teeth.

'When I heard the lock turn,' he said in a quavering voice, 'it scared the crap out of me. I thought I'd be safe here for a few days.' He turned away from me and dropped like a dead body into one of the lounging chairs. The gun slipped out of his fingers and thudded on to Sydney's two-hundred-year-old Persian carpet. Fel put a filthy hand across his eyes and began to weep.

I closed the door, then walked unsteadily across to the liquor cabinet. With shaking hands I poured two stiff whiskies.

'Take it easy,' I said and put one of the glasses on the occasional table by his side. 'Pull yourself together. Drink this.'

He looked up at me, rubbing his face with the back of his hand. There was a desperate, animal expression in his eyes that warned me how dangerous he was.

161

'You bastard!' he said, his voice shaking. 'You got me into this with your smooth talk! You're damn well going to get me out of it!'

I drank half the whisky, then walking to a chair near his, I sat down.

'Where's Rhea?' I asked.

He clenched his fists and banged the sides of his head. I could see he was hysterical with fear and this gave me confidence.

'Fel! Pull yourself together! Where's Rhea?'

'Don't talk to me about that bitch!' He now began to pound his fist on his knees. 'You've got to help me! You got me into this! I saw the papers . . . they want me for murder!'

Seeing his panic, hearing him talk, seeing he was way out with fear, I felt I could handle him.

'I'll help you, but I must know what happened. Where's Rhea?'

He began crying again: sobs shaking him. I took a long pull at the whisky, then sat back, watching him. His craven fear and his filth disgusted me.

I let him sob on. Finally, he couldn't squeeze out any more tears and wiping his eyes on the heel of his wrist, he looked blearily at me.

'If they catch me, they'll put me away for twenty years,' he gasped, each word jerking out of him. 'I couldn't stand that! I'm not built like that! Twenty years behind bars! They'll never take me alive!'

'Stop thinking about yourself,' I said, 'where's Rhea?'

'The bitch! My goddamn sister.' He stood up, shook his fists above his head, then sat down again. He was behaving like a crazy man. 'The guns weren't loaded! I swear it! She must have loaded them! You said not to load them and I didn't load them! She did it! She killed the queer! She tried to kill you! You know it! You must tell the fuzz I hadn't anything to do with it!'

'Where's Rhea?' I said.

'You don't believe me, do you? You think I'm as bad as she is, don't you? I'm not! She's always been a curse to me! I should never have taken her back! I should never have listened to your smooth talk! Twenty years behind bars! I couldn't take it!'

'What are you doing here?' I said quietly, hoping the sound of my voice might calm him.

He leaned back in the chair, holding his head in his hands.

'Don't ask goddamn questions! I want to get out of here! I want money! I want a car! I've got to get out of this goddamn place!'

'I'll give you money,' I said. 'I'll help you get away. I'll get you a car.'

He stared at me. He was shivering, but now there was a gleam of hope in his eyes.

'You'd better!' he said huskily. 'You and your goddamn millions! This has been a sweet thing for you, hasn't it?'

That was his mistake. I was beginning to feel sorry for him, but by saying that, he killed any feeling of pity I might have had for him.

'I said I would help you,' I said.

'How could she have killed that queer?' he said, staring down at his dirty hands. 'She's rotten! You know what she did to me ... me ... her brother?' He looked up, his eyes loaded with misery. 'We chased out of this goddamn place. She had the necklace. We got in the car. She drove. We went like bats out of hell to the highway. I was cursing her for shooting, but she didn't even look at me. I thought we were heading for Miami. I left it all to her: all I could do was to curse her. When we got on to the swamp road through the mangrove forest—you know?—just outside the city, she stood on the brakes. I was pissing myself, looking back to see if the fuzz were after us. I yelled at her to keep going. I can see her now.' Again he thumped his knees with his clenched fists. 'Her goddamn eyes were like ice chips. 'Rear tyre, off-side is flat,' she said. 'Get out and check.' So I got out and checked. Okay, so I'm a dope: so I buy anything, like I bought your smooth talk. I hadn't even reached the back of the car before the bitch was away with all those diamonds ... not caring a goddamn what happened ... to me.' His voice broke and he began to cry again, rocking himself to and fro in his misery.

I lit a cigarette. I was no longer frightened of him, although I knew he was still dangerous. If the police got him, he would talk.

Looking at him, I came to a cold-blooded decision. He had to be silenced. There was no other solution if I were to remain safe.

I sat there, smoking and looking at him as he snivelled and cried. His dirt, his smell, his craven spirit made him no more important to me than a fly on the wall.

The City Hall clock struck twelve.

'You must be hungry, Fel,' I said. 'I'll get you something to eat.'

He stopped snivelling.

'Hungry? I'm bloody starving! The time I've had! I've been living on raw fish and crabs in that goddamn swamp! You ever been in there? The stinking place is full of snakes and alligators!'

I telephoned the restaurant and asked the maître d' to send up the lunch.

'Go out on the terrace, Fel, and keep out of sight.'

He grabbed up his glass of whisky, drained it, then went out on to the terrace.

I took his glass into the kitchen, my mind busy. How to silence him? I realised I was planning to murder him, but the thought didn't shock me. If I could get rid of him and then get rid of Rhea I would be safe, and not only safe, but the world would truly be at my feet.

I returned to the sitting-room and sat down. During the quarter of an hour's wait until the waiter appeared, an idea began to form in my mind. It seemed to me that Fel could be easily dealt with, but not Rhea. Well, one bridge at the time, I told myself.

The waiter came in, wheeling a trolley. He beamed at me.

'Morning, Mr. Carr. Good to see you again. There's a bottle of champagne with the maître d's compliments. The chef has given you his special for today.'

I tipped him two dollars and when he had gone, I went out

on to the terrace where Fel was sitting with his back against the balustrade, his knees drawn up to his chin.

'Come and get it,' I said.

He shoved past me, went to the table and stared at the food, then he sat down and began to eat. He ate like a starving pig, stuffing food into his mouth, bolting it down, making choking noises. He so sickened me, I went out on to the terrace and waited there until he had finished, but while waiting, I went over the plan in my mind: the plan to get rid of him for good and in safety.

Hearing a loud belch, I decided he had finished eating and I returned to the sitting-room.

God knows what the waiter would think when he came to collect the trolley, I thought as I looked at the debris. Fel had spilt food on the table cloth; there was nothing left from the copious cheese board; the basket that had contained six rolls of bread was empty. There were wine stains not only on the table-cloth, but also on the immaculate cloth that covered the trolley. Even the fruit basket was empty.

Never mind, I told myself, a ten-dollar tip would put this right.

I looked at Fel who was lighting a cigarette.

'Man!' he said. 'Do you rich creeps know how to live! That was the best goddamn meal I've ever eaten!'

'You must have been hungry,' I said.

'Yeah ... you sitting in this plush joint and me out there in the dark with snakes.' He stared at me, his eyes hating me. 'Well, buster, you got me into this mess ... you get me out of it or I'll fix you! If the cops catch up with me, I'll sing. You and me will go away for twenty goddamn years!'

He didn't know it but he was talking himself into death.

'How did you get into this apartment, Fel?' I asked, sitting down and lighting a cigarette.

'Any punk could get in here. That wasn't so tough. Never mind that ... I want a car and I want money.'

'You can take my car. It's parked outside. How much money do you want?'

He squinted at me.

'Fifty grand.'

I nodded.

'I can manage that. What are your plans, Fel?'

'I'll drive to Key West. I have a pal who'll get me to Cuba.
Once there, I'll send you my address.' He leered at me and I
could see the whisky was hitting him. 'Then you'll send me
five hundred grand. That'll be my final pay off. When I get it,
you won't ever hear from me again.'

'But I could hear from Rhea,' I said.

'That's your funeral. I'm talking for myself. She's got the
necklace so why should she worry you? I've got nothing!'

'Where is she, Fel?'

'What's it to you? You leave her alone. She's poison! Forget her ... she'll sell the necklace and she'll fade. Forget her.'

I tipped more whisky into his glass. He grinned and picking
up the glass, he drained it.

'Man! Do you bastards live well!' He reached for the
whisky bottle and poured more spirit into his glass. 'My goddamn sister! You know something, buster? She doesn't give a
goddamn for anyone except this creep of hers. What a punk!
What a goddamn piss-pot! I bet right now she's having it off
with him! That stinker really turns her on!'

'Using my car, Fel, you won't have any trouble,' I said. 'As
soon as it's dark ... after ten o'clock, all you have to do is to
get in the car and take off.'

He half shut his eyes. I could see he was pretty drunk.

'How about the money?'

'That's no problem. I have it right here.'

He peered at me. I could see he was having trouble in focus-
ing me.

'Right here?'

'Yes.'

'Who do you think you're conning? Let's see it.'

'You'll see it. Who is this creep Rhea's with?'

He blew out his cheeks.

'Who cares for a stick of crap like Spooky?' He giggled.
'Boy! What a creep! Just proves what a stupid bitch she is to

get turned on by a stinker like him ... he's ten years younger than she is.'

'Spooky Jinx?' I asked.

'Yeah ... you know him?'

'I ran into him in Luceville ... quite a character.'

'You can say that again.' He leaned back. 'Woe! That was some meal!'

'How come Rhea has hooked up with Spooky?'

'You tell me! She was having it off with him before she went to jail. As soon as she comes out, she chases after him. Nuts! A creep like that!' He frowned, shook his head, then rubbed his dirty hands across his eyes. 'I guess I've drunk too much ... wanna sleep.'

'Go ahead,' I said. 'Have a sleep.'

An animal instinct brought him upright.

'Show me the money, buster. You say you have it here ... show it to me.'

This was it.

'It's in the safe.' I got to my feet.

'Safe ... what safe?'

I walked over to the Picasso picture, lifted it off the wall, revealing the safe.

'Well, for hell's sake!' Fel lurched to his feet. 'Never thought of looking there! You got money in that can?'

'That's where it is.'

'Go ahead, buster ... open it!'

I twisted the dial, knowing that by doing so, I was setting off an alarm at police headquarters.

'I'm not too sure how to open it,' I said. 'I have the combination, but it's tricky.'

'So it's tricky,' Fel said, breathing whisky fumes down my neck as he stared at the dial. 'So go ahead and open it.'

I spun the knob, clicking up the numbers, knowing by now a prowl car would be on the way.

'Two-double-one, five-double-eight, six-double-nine,' I muttered as I flicked the dial around. This was not the combination which, because of poor Sydney's hopeless memory was a simple 1—2—3 told to me by Tom Luce. I pulled the knob, then shook my head. 'Must have made a slip. Here, Fel, you try ... I'll call the numbers.'

'Me? I'm goddamn drunk!' He lurched against me, sending me staggering. 'You open it! Come on, you punk! You damn well open it.'

I began to move the dial around. How long would I have to wait before the police arrived? I began to sweat.

'Two-double-one-five-double-eight,' I intoned, moving the dial. 'Six-double nine. That's it.' I pulled at the knob. 'Well, for God's sake!'

'Can't you open it?' Fel's voice was a snarl. 'You conning me?'

'That's the combination,' I said. 'Why the hell won't it open?'

Then the telephone bell rang.

We both turned and looked at the telephone. Leaving Fel, I took two quick strides, lifted the receiver and said, 'Hello ... yes?'

'Mr. Carr? This is Harry. I've two police officers here. Are you all right up there.'

'No ... you have a wrong number,' I said and hung up.

I turned to see Fel lurch across the room and pick up his gun.

'A wrong number?' he said, squinting at me.

'Yes.'

We stared at each other.

'You aren't trying to con me, you bastard?'

'Oh, shut up!' I crossed to the safe, my heart thumping. As I began to turn the dial yet again, the front door bell buzzed.

I turned around and looked at Fel who was motionless, staring through the open door of the living-room into the lobby.

'Open up!' a tough voice snapped. 'Police!'

Fel lifted his gun and pointed it at me.

'You bastard!'

'Quick! Out on to the terrace ... I'll stall them!' I moved by him, my body cringing ... would he shoot?

The bell buzzed again.

I was out on the terrace. Fel followed me.

'You can get down ... quick! Take my car. I'll keep them talking.'

Shivering, his mouth working, Fel leaned far over the balustrade to look at the balcony below. I moved up behind him, then hooking my fingers into the cuffs of his trousers, I heaved up.

He gave a scream of terror and his gun went off, then he plunged down into space as I heard the front door burst open.

It had been so easy, I thought as I drove up the freeway, heading for Luceville ... so absurdly easy.

Now I had made one big step forward: one mouth silenced. Now for Rhea ...

Sergeant Hess had come to the penthouse and he had questioned me, but I knew by his manner and by the way he treated me he thought I was lucky to be alive.

I told him that when I had let myself into the apartment, I had realised that someone was in there but before I could get out Morgan had appeared, gun in hand. He had threatened to shoot me if I raised the alarm. I explained how he had started drinking and had become garrulous ... how he had told me he had been living in the mangrove swamp and was starving. He had demanded food and I had got him a meal from the restaurant. After he had eaten, he had demanded money. This, I said, was my chance. I knew Sydney's safe was wired to police headquarters. When the police arrived, Morgan had panicked. He had rushed out on to the terrace and had tried to climb to the lower balcony. I had tried to stop him. He had fired at me, then lost his hold and had fallen.

All this added up when Hess went over the penthouse. There were signs that Morgan had slept over-night and his filthy hand-prints were everywhere.

'Well, we know now he and his sister are the two,' Hess had said. 'Now, we have to find her.'

But not before I do, I told myself. I went on to tell him how Rhea had ditched her brother and had made off with the necklace.

Here was my chance to confuse the hunt and I took it.

'Morgan said they planned to drive to Key West and they had a friend there who could get them to Cuba. He was sure Rhea was heading for Key West when she ditched him.'

Hess grimaced.

'Cuba! If she's there ... we've lost her.'

The newspapers gave Fel's death a big play. I was sure Rhea would read about it, but she wouldn't know that Fel had told me about Spooky Jinx. Maybe she wasn't holed up in his pad, but it was worth a try. I had to silence her. I would have no future unless she was dead.

I waited until Fel's inquest was over and then I told Hess I was going to 'Frisco for a change of scene. He asked me to keep in touch with him. If they caught up with Rhea, I would be the principal witness, but from his expression, I got the impression he now hadn't much hope of finding her.

Before leaving Paradise City for Luceville, I called Claude, Sydney's manservant. I asked him if he would work for me, explaining I was moving into the penthouse.

'I appreciate the offer, Mr. Larry,' he said, 'but I could never work for any other gentleman after working for Mr. Sydney. But if it would be helpful, I will try to find someone reliable for you.'

'Don't bother,' I said, and hung up.

To be turned down by a fat, elderly queer soured me. I would have paid him as much as Sydney had paid him ... who the hell did he think he was?

Then thinking about it, I saw his point. Why should he want to work for anyone now? Hadn't Sydney taken care of him handsomely? But I knew this wasn't the real reason. I knew Claude despised me for moving into Sydney's home ... as I was beginning to despise myself.

Three days after Fel's inquest, I got in the Buick and headed for Luceville.

The previous day I had driven to Miami and had bought myself a hippy outfit: a flowered shirt, jeans and black sneakers. I had gone to one of the waterfront hock shops and had bought a .38 police special automatic with a box of slugs. I then went to a gimmick shop and bought a black, candy floss wig, a broad belt with a miniature skull for a buckle and a flick knife.

Back in my apartment, I made a solution of earth, oil and water, taking the earth from the flower boxes on my terrace, and thoroughly dirtied the shirt and jeans.

Twenty miles from Luceville, I stopped at a small town and garaged the Buick, then carrying a suitcase containing the hippy outfit I went along to a used car lot and bought a battered Chevvy.

On a lonely stretch of beach, I changed into the hippy outfit, and put on the candy floss wig. I hadn't shaved for three days and now, looking at myself in the driving mirror, I decided I could walk past even Jenny without her recognizing me.

I was now ready to go.

I sat behind the driving wheel and stared through the dusty windshield and took stock.

I had no feeling of remorse for Fel Morgan. I was sure he would have blackmailed me for the rest of my days. I had no qualms for what I was planning to do with Rhea if I found her ... it was my life or hers.

But I knew it wasn't going to be easy. She might not be holed up with Spooky, although I had a feeling she was, and even if she was, I had to trap her and then kill her.

Trapping and killing her would be as dangerous and as difficult as trapping and killing a wild cat.

But it had to be done.

TEN

I drove into Luceville as the City Hall clock struck six. Because of the smog and the cement dust I drove as other drivers were doing with dipped headlights. I felt the dust gritty around my collar and it gave me a feeling of nostalgia.

To reach Spooky's pad on Lexington I had to cross the centre of the city and I got snarled up in the home-going traffic.

As I crawled past Jenny's office block I wondered if she was up there on the sixth floor, her hair untidy as she scribbled on a yellow form. But this was no time to think of Jenny. The time to think of her, I told myself, was when I knew for certain I was safe. Until then, she must remain like something one urgently longs for but knows one can't afford.

I dumped the Chevvy in a parking lot within easy walking distance of Lexington, then taking my hold-all, containing a spare shirt, shaving kit and the .38 automatic, I walked through the slums until I came to Lexington.

It was dark now and the street lights were on. Apart from a few old drunks, sitting on trash bins, a few coloured kids kicking a ball around in the street, Lexington at this hour was deserted.

Opposite No. 245: Spooky's pad was a dilapidated four-storey tenement house. Two snot-nosed, dirty, white kids sat on the steps. With their grimy little fists clenched between their knees, their tiny shoulders hunched, they stared, for something better to do, at the collection of filth lying in the gutter: it included a dead cat.

On the transom above the battered front door was written:

172

Rooms. Vacancies

This seemed to me to be too good to be true. I paused to look across the street at No. 245, then started up the steps, moving around the kids who squinted up at me, their tragic little eyes suspicious. I entered a lobby that smelt of urine, stale body sweat and cats.

An old biddy stood in an open doorway, digging with a splinter of wood at what she had left of her teeth. What hair she had was greasy rats' tails. Her cover-all was stiff with dirt. She couldn't have been less than eighty, probably more.

I paused before her. She took me in from the candy floss wig down to my scuffed sneakers. I could see by her sneering expression she didn't like what she saw.

'You got a room, Ma?' I said, putting down the hold-all.

'Don't call me Ma, you young bastard,' she said in a voice thick with phlegm. 'Mrs. Reynolds to you and don't you forget it.'

'Okay, Mrs. Reynolds. You got a room?'

'Twelve bucks a week, paid in advance.'

'Let's take a gander.'

I knew the dialogue was strictly from a B movie and from her sneer she knew it too.

'Second floor. Number five. The key's in the lock.'

I walked up the creaky uncovered stairs, not touching the filthy banister rail to the second floor. Number five was at the end of a smelly corridor.

The room was about ten-feet square. It contained a bed, a table, two hardbacked chairs, a closet and a threadbare carpet. The wallpaper was peeling by the window. There was a grease covered bench on which stood a gas ring.

Leaving my hold-all, I went down the stairs, paid the old biddy twelve dollars, then walked to an Italian store where I bought enough groceries to last me a few days. To the various cans of food, I added a bottle of whisky. Then I went to a hardware store and bought a small saucepan and a frying-pan.

Mrs Reynolds was still propping up her doorway when I returned.

'Where do I wash?' I asked.

She eyed me, scratched under her left armpit, then said, 'Public baths at the end of the street. There's a crapper on every floor. What more do you want?'

I carried my purchases up to the room, shut and locked the door, set everything down on the table, then examined the bed. The sheets were clean enough, but the two thin blankets carried suspicious looking stains. I wondered when the bugs would appear.

A change of scene?

I thought of Sydney's luxurious penthouse which I had inherited. This ghastly little room was something I had to endure if I were to keep the penthouse and Sydney's millions.

Turning off the light, I pulled a chair to the window and began my watch. There were eighteen dirty windows facing me across the street: five of them showing lights. One of these windows belonged to Spooky. I had no idea which of the eighteen was his, but sooner or later, if I watched long enough, I would spot him.

I sat there, smoking and watching. People moved in the lighted squares of their windows: most of them young, wearing way-out gear. On the fifth floor, third window to the left, a handsome young Negress wearing only stretch pants was jiggling to a soundless radio, cupping her naked breasts in her hands. Watching her, I felt lust stir and forced my eyes away from her.

Around 2000 I got hungry. I left the window, pulled down the blind and turned on the light. While I was heating a can of beans I heard the roar of an approaching motor bike. Turning off the gas and the light, I moved fast to the window and pulled aside the blind. There was Spooky astride a glittering new Honda, pulling up outside No. 245.

I watched him as he climbed off the machine and strutted up the steps leading to his pad.

This was the moment. I watched him disappear into the darkness of the block, then I waited for a light to come on in one of the darkened windows. While I waited, I watched the Negress who had put on a flowered shirt and was stirring some-

174

thing in a saucepan.

After a fifteen minute wait, I realised that in whichever room Spooky lived the light was already on when he entered for no light came up in any of the darkened windows. Did that mean that Rhea was in Spooky's pad? Why not? Why should she sit in the darkness? I began to examine each lighted window. Three of them were without curtains and I could see who were in the rooms. The two remaining windows had flimsy curtains, but not flimsy enough to see through. One was on the third floor. The other on the top floor immediately above the room occupied by the Negress. It seemed to me that one of these rooms must be Spooky's.

I dropped the blind, put on the light and re-heated the beans. For a start this first day hadn't been bad. I was making progress. At least I now knew Spooky either lived on the third or top floor of this block.

I ate the beans, then turning off the light and raising the blind, I sat again before the window.

Around 2100 the light in the window on the third floor went out. I now concentrated my attention on the lighted window on the top floor. I watched for almost an hour, then suddenly a shadow moved across the curtains. I recognised Spooky's silhouette. It was unmistakable. If I hadn't been watching continuously I would have missed this fleeting shadow. So he was on the top floor, but was Rhea up there with him?

I sat there, watching. The lights in the various windows began to go out. The Negress picked up a large handbag, went to her door and flicked up the light switch. Finally, the only light in the building came through the windows of Spooky's pad.

Then I saw him come running down the steps and get astride his Honda. The machine burst into an ear-splitting roar. Clapping his helmet on his greasy head, he took off, but the light in his window remained on.

This could mean either of two things: either Spooky didn't give a damn about his electricity bill or else Rhea was up there in hiding.

But how to find out?

I was a stranger in the district. It would be too dangerous to wander into Spooky's block even though it looked now that everyone had left the building.

I lit a cigarette and surveyed the street below. Like rats appearing when darkness falls, the street was becoming active. Elderly ragged men and women came shuffling down the steps of the various tenement blocks in search of a bar.

Then I saw the Negress. She was leaning against the rusty railings, swinging her large handbag and I then knew what she was—a prostitute.

I knew her room was immediately below Spooky's pad. Here was my chance. Maybe I could get confirmation that Rhea was up there.

I thought of the Negress as I had seen her dancing, half naked, in her room. She was pretty and beautifully made. I hadn't had sex since I had met Judy: that seemed a long, long time ago.

Pushing back the chair, I stood up, groped my way across the dark room to the door and moved out into the smelly corridor.

On my way down the stairs I met no one. Mrs. Reynold's door was shut. Through the thin panels came the sound of a TV set. I lounged down the steps into the cement-dusty night. The street's flotsam—youths, girls, drunks and old people—swirled around me. I looked across the street at the Negress who had spotted me. She was looking towards me. I waited until two beat-up cars had roared past me, then crossed the street.

She was moving towards me as I reached the opposite side walk. 'Hi, honey,' she said softly, her white teeth gleaming in the lamp light. 'Lonely?'

I stood by her, looking at her. Her skin was the colour of milky coffee. Her ironed-out black hair framed her face. Even the importance of finding Rhea and silencing her went out of my mind. I had to get this repression that had built up in my body purged.

'You can say that again,' I said huskily. 'Let's do something about it.'

She surveyed me, her big, black eyes probing.

'It'll cost you ten bucks, honey,' she said. 'You got ten bucks?'

I thought of my offer to Rhea of five hundred dollars.

'I've got it,' I said.

'You don't look as if you have two bucks.' She smiled at me. 'You're new around here, aren't you?'

I dug into my hip pocket and showed her a ten-dollar bill. Her slim brown fingers snapped the bill out of my fingers the way a lizard nails a fly.

'Let's go, honey,' she said. 'It's all action from now on.'

She led me into the tenement block that smelt worse than my block. She wriggled her bottom at me as she climbed the stairs with me just behind her. It was a long climb and by the time I reached her landing I had a hard-on that really hurt.

She acted up to me and it was good. In the past when I couldn't be bothered to chase after some girl, I had taken a tart. I had never had value for money. Usually they lay staring up at the ceiling, some even smoking, most of them giggling but this little Negress did an act that made me feel I was stirring her, although I knew I wasn't.

When it was over and I had rolled away from her, she didn't do what most of them did—slide off the bed and begin dressing. She lay by my side, reached for a pack of cigarettes, lit two and gave me one.

'You certainly wanted that, honey,' she said, cupping her breasts in her hands.

Yes, I had certainly wanted it. Now I felt completely relaxed as if a boil that had been tormenting me had burst. I dragged smoke down into my lungs and stared up at the dirty ceiling. Then I became aware of footsteps overhead. I had been in such a state before I had laid this girl everything had gone out of focus. Now I heard these footsteps . . . click-click-click of a woman's heels, pounding over my head. Then I remembered Rhea and why I was in this sordid little room with a young, naked Negress lying by my side.

I listened.

Backwards and forwards this woman walked above my

head: non-stop. Click-click-click.

The Negress crushed out her cigarette.

'I've got to get back to work now, honey,' she said. 'Did you have a good time?'

'What goes on up there?' I said and pointed to the ceiling.

'Why should you worry?' She sat up and swung her long legs off the bed. 'Up on your feet, honey. I have to go to work.'

I put my arm around her slim waist and pulled her against me.

'No hurry . . . another ten dollars buys me your time.'

She spread her warm body down on mine.

'You mean that?'

'Want the money now?'

'Always now, honey. I have to live.'

I got off the bed, went over to where I had left my pants, found another ten-dollar bill and handed it to her. As I laid down, she threw her leg across me and began to nibble at my ear. I let her work on me while I listened to the footsteps moving across the ceiling.

'What goes on up there?' I asked. 'Sounds like a marathon.'

'A nutter.' The Negress began to stroke the back of my neck. 'She drives me crazy. Day after day, night after night, she walks. If it wasn't for Spooky, I'd go up there and bawl her out, but she's Spooky's piece and he's a big noise in this craphouse.'

'Have you seen her?'

She lifted herself on her elbow and stared down at me, her big, black eyes quizzing.

'Why the questions, honey? Let's have some action.'

All the time she was speaking, I could hear the footsteps.

'Spooky's girl?'

'You know Spooky?'

'I know him for the bastard he is.'

She relaxed and lowered herself on me again.

'They're in trouble up there. He's hiding her from the fuzz,' she mumbled, her lips against my neck. 'She's been holed up there for two weeks—never goes out: just walks the goddamn floor and drives me crazy.'

I now knew all I wanted to know. I had found Rhea!

Back in my own sordid room, I lay on the bed with the light off and the curtains drawn back. The street lights gave me enough light to see. I was relaxed: this sexual experience had been something I had really needed. Sadie—the Negress had told me her name when I was leaving—had done a thorough therapeutic job on me.

I now knew that Rhea was in Spooky's pad. As long as she remained alive my own freedom and my inheritance from Sydney were in jeopardy. If the police caught her, she would talk, implicating me. I had to silence her—but how?

Then an alarming thought dropped into my mind. Had she told Spooky about me? If I silenced her would Spooky then appear on my horizon to blackmail me? Had she told him she had a diamond necklace worth, as she imagined, over a million dollars? Would she give a slob like Spooky such a dangerous piece of information? This was something I had to find out. If she had told him then I would have a double killing on my hands. I would have to silence both of them. I didn't flinch at the thought. I felt neither Rhea nor Spooky had any right to live. To me, they were dangerous animals and I the hunter, but if I could avoid a double killing it would be easier and safer for me.

Still thinking, still planning, I dozed off, but around two o'clock the first of the bugs arrived. I spent the rest of the night sitting on a hard-backed chair, my head on my arms, across the table.

Soon after 0300, the silence of the night was split by the roar of a motorcycle. I stood at the window and watched Spooky swagger up the steps and to his pad.

After eating a poor breakfast the following morning, I went along to the public baths. The rest of the morning I spent wandering the streets, keeping away from the centre of the town. I was fearful of running into Jenny. I bought a box of anti-bug powder and returned to my room to prepare a lunch of canned beef and canned potatoes. After smothering the bedding and the mattress with the powder, I lay down and went to sleep.

I woke at 1900. Going to the window, I looked across the street to see a light showing behind the curtains of Spooky's pad. Sadie, in the room below was cooking something at her stove. Looking down at the street, I saw the Honda was gone which meant Spooky had gone out.

I looked through the cans of food I had bought, decided to try the ravioli which turned out to be tough and tasteless. Then I sat by the window, smoking until around 2100 I saw Sadie leave her room.

I went over to my hold-all and took from it the .38 automatic which I slid into my hip pocket, then I went down on to the street and joined Sadie as she came from the block.

'Hi, sugar,' I said. 'How about some more action?'

She smiled at me. 'You sure are keen, man.' She linked her arm in mine. 'Yeah . . . let's have some action.'

Up in her room, I took a hundred-dollar bill from my pocket and let her see it.

'Do you want to earn this, Sadie?'

Her eyes popped wide open.

'You want some kinky stuff?'

'I want to spend the night here,' I said. 'I've got bugs in my room.'

She put her head on one side, her eyes quizzing.

'Where do you get all this beautiful bread from, honey?'

'Never mind. Do I sleep here or do I go to a hotel?'

She held out her hand.

'Give . . . you sleep right here.'

When I had entered the room I had become aware of Rhea still pacing.

'Your nutter keeps walking,' I said, giving Sadie the bill.

'You can say that again. I'm used to it now. It's when she stops that it gets me.'

I watched her put the bill into her handbag, then she went over to the bed. She stripped the bedding. Going to a closet, she produced clean sheets.

'Nothing but the best,' I said as I joined her to help re-make the bed.

'When a honey pays a hundred bucks, he's entitled to clean sheets,' Sadie said. 'As we have the night before us, I'm taking a shower. You want a drink or some food?'

'I'll take a drink.'

She produced a bottle of cheap whisky, charge-water and ice, then left me while she took a shower.

I sat in a beat-up armchair and listened to Rhea walk the floor above my head. She sounded like a caged animal. I thought of her, remembering the time when I had lusted for her, but now she meant nothing to me except a dangerous animal. If I had dared to have done it, I would have gone up there, kicked the door open and shot her, but I knew that wasn't the safe way to play out this little drama. When I did kill her, I had to be sure the killing could never be pinned on me.

My love making with Sadie was much more gentle this time: the urgency had gone. We went to sleep, twined in each other's arms.

Sadie slept deeply, but I just hovered between sleep and wakefulness. I half listened to the click-click-click as Rhea continued to pace, then I became fully awake when the roar of the approaching Honda shook the window.

Sadie moaned and moved, then turned over and went back to sleep.

Below, a door slammed violently. Then I heard heavy footfalls as Spooky pounded up the stairs. The click-click-click of Rhea's heels suddenly stopped. I heard Spooky open his door, then slam it shut.

'Listen, you bitch, this is the last goddamn bottle of whisky I'm buying!'

His deep menacing voice came through the ceiling as if he was in Sadie's room.

'Give it to me!' I immediately recognised Rhea's voice.

'Take it! Drink yourself to death! Why the hell should I care?'

Sadie moaned softly in her sleep.

There was a long pause, then Spooky started to talk again:

'I've had enough of this! I want you out! I want my pad to myself! I want you out!'

'Shut up, you stupid jerk of a bastard!' There was a hysterical note in Rhea's voice that alerted me. 'I'm staying here! I've nowhere else to go! You start trouble for me, you goddamn creep and I'll fix you! I can fix you, Spooky! The fuzz can't wait to get their paws on you!'

After a long pause, Spooky said, 'Just what the hell is all this? I've got to know! What's this about you staying here until the heat cools off? What heat? What have you done? Why the hell do you come here, hiding from the fuzz? Where's Fel? I want to know! I've had enough of you walking the goddamn floor and swilling whisky. I want my pad back without you!'

'Do you?' Lying motionless, feeling Sadie's body warmth seeping through me as she pressed against me, I listened. Rhea went on. 'I stay here until it's safe for me to go. I'm not showing myself on the streets until the heat's off. I've done a lot for you. Who bought your goddamn bike? Why don't you try to earn something? What are you good for except riding a bike and bragging, you stupid, brainless creep?'

'Okay.' Spooky's voice went down a tone and I had to listen hard to hear what he was saying. 'Then you get out! Go ahead and talk to the fuzz about me. They won't worry me once they get you. So pack and get out!'

'Have a drink, Spooky.'

'I said . . . get out!'

'Aw, come on . . . let's forget it. We're always fighting.' There was a sudden whine in Rhea's voice. 'Have a drink, I want bed . . . and you.'

'Who wants you? I said get out!'

'I know you did, honey, but I want bed. Come on.'

'I've had enough of you, you drunken cow! Go fix your own goddamn problems and leave me alone!'

I suddenly realised by the viciousness in his voice that he meant what he was saying. I slid off the bed and struggled into my clothes. This could be my chance! She hadn't told him! So Spooky wasn't a menace to me! As I pulled on my shoes,

Sadie turned on her back.

'Honey ... where are you?' she muttered and then went back to sleep.

I heard Spooky yell: 'Out!'

The door above slammed open: there was a thud.

'Take your goddamn junk!' Another thud, then the door slammed shut.

By this time I was out in the corridor. I shut Sadie's door softly, then ran down the stairs to the entrance of the block. I stood against the wall in the darkness, listening.

Rhea started down the stairs. I heard her muttering, 'Bastard ... Bastard.'

Then I saw her outline as she groped her way across the lobby to where I was standing.

'Take it easy, baby,' I said softly. 'There's a fuzz passing.'

She came to an abrupt stop, catching her breath. She peered at me.

'Who the hell are you?'

'Like you ... trying to cool off,' I said.

She slumped against the wall by my side. I could smell the whisky on her breath.

'Cooling off? What do you mean?' Her words were slurred. She was higher than a kite.

'I heard. Want to run with me, baby? I've a car. I know a pad out of town that's safe.'

She slid down on the floor.

'God! I'm drunk!' There was a wail of despair in her voice. 'I want to die!'

But not here, I thought. The bang of my gun would start trouble for me. I had to get her out in the open before I shot her.

'Come on, baby,' I said, and taking hold of her arm, I hauled her to her feet. 'Let's go.'

She leaned against me.

'Who are you? I can't see you. Who the hell are you?'

'Come on ... let's go.'

I hauled her down the steps and on to the deserted street. She staggered as she walked and I had to steady her. Under the street light, she pulled away from me and we looked at each other. I scarcely knew her. She had aged horribly. There were streaks of white in her red hair. Her emerald green eyes glowed as if light bulbs were behind them. She was emaciated. She weaved as she peered at me.

She had on the blood-red trouser suit and she carried a bulging sling bag on her shoulder.

'Hi, Wig-top,' she said. 'You got any hair under that wig?'

'Come on, baby,' I said. 'I've a car up the street. Let's you and me take off.'

She studied me drunkenly. The candy floss wig, my thick beard, my dirty clothes seemed to give her confidence.

'You on the run too?'

'I'll say. Let's go.'

She laughed: a horrible hysterical drunken sound.

'My brother died,' she said. 'The only goddamn sonofabitch who understood me. The fuzz killed him.'

I took hold of her arm.

'Let's get the hell out of here.'

She went with me. She was so drunk she would have fallen flat on her face if I hadn't held on to her.

We weaved together down the deserted street and to where I had parked the Chevvy. As I unlocked the car door, she leaned against the car, staring at me.

'Haven't I seen you before, Wig-top?'

'What do the fuzz want you for?' I asked and slid into the driving seat.

'Why the hell should you care?'

'That's right ... you getting in or staying out?'

She opened the offside door and dropped into the passenger's seat. I had to lean across her to slam the door.

'Where are we going, Wig-top?'

'I don't know where you are going, but I know where I'm going. I'm heading for the coast. My brother has a boat. He's going to take me to Havana.'

'Havana?' She pressed her hands to her face. 'I want to get there.'

'So okay ... have you any money?'

She slapped her big bag.

'It's here. Come on, Wig-top, let's get moving.'

When we got onto the Tamiami Trial, heading for Naples, she fell asleep.

The time now was 0400. In another hour it would be light. The broad freeway was deserted. On either side were dense forests of Cypress and pine trees.

I looked at her. Her head was against the window, her eyes closed. All I had to do was to slow down, bring the car to a gentle stop, take the .38 from my hip pocket, shoot her through the head, open the offside door and tip her body on to the road, then drive off. There was nothing to it. Just before reaching Naples, I'd get rid of the candy floss wig, dump the car and catch a Greyhound bus to Sarasota. There I'd buy a new outfit, shave off my beard and head across country by bus to Fort Pierce. From there, by bus I'd head back to Little Jackson where I had garaged my Buick. Then I would drive back to Paradise City: free and safe!

This plan flashed through my mind: it was so easy. I had imagined getting rid of Rhea would have been impossibly dangerous, but there she was in a drunken sleep entirely at my mercy. All I had to do was to point the gun at her and squeeze the trigger.

I looked into the driving mirror. The long freeway was dark: no sign of approaching headlights. Gently, I eased my foot off the gas pedal. The car began to lose speed, then drifted slowly to a standstill in the deep shadows of an oak tree as I shifted the gear lever into neutral. I set the handbrake.

I looked at Rhea, but she still slept, then I put my hand behind me and my fingers closed over the butt of the .38. Slowly, I drew the gun and slid back the safety catch.

I lifted the gun and pointed it at her head, my finger curling around the trigger, but that was a far as I went.

I sat there, looking at her, the gun aiming at her and in despair, I knew I couldn't pull the trigger. I couldn't kill her in cold blood. In the heat of the moment I had killed Fel, but it wasn't in my make-up to shoot a sleeping woman.

Rhea's eyes suddenly snapped open.

'Go ahead, Larry Carr,' she said. 'Prove to yourself you have some guts. Go ahead ... kill me!'

The blazing headlights of an approaching truck lit up the interior of the Chevvy. I could see Rhea clearly. God! She looked awful! How I could have ever lusted for her seemed now, looking at her, to be some dreadful erotic nightmare. She was huddled in the corner, her eyes dull, her thin lips twisted into a sneering little grin and she looked out of her mind.

'Go ahead ... kill me!' she repeated.

The truck roared by, shaking the Chevvy in its slipstream. The thought flashed through my mind, making me flinch, that if I had killed her, the truck would have passed as I was tipping her body on to the road.

I let the gun slip out of my hand. It dropped on the bench seat between us. I knew this was the end of the road for me and I suddenly didn't care anymore.

'What's the matter, Cheapie?' she asked. 'You had it all planned, didn't you? Run out of guts? Did you imagine I wouldn't know you even in that godawful wig?'

I stared at her, hating her. She was as repulsive to me as a leper.

'I'll say what your boy friend said to you: "Get out!"' I said. 'Get out of my car.'

She peered at me.

'Don't get your bowels in an uproar. I've got the necklace ... you and I could still beat the rap.' She fumbled in her bag, opened it and took out the leather jewel case. 'Look ... I have it! A million dollars! You said you could sell it! Together, we can go to Havana. We could start a new life together.'

Together? With her? I shuddered.

'Sell it? Live with you?' I said. 'I wouldn't live with you if you were the last whore left in the world! That necklace isn't worth a dime ... it's a fake.'

She stiffened and leaned forward. Her green eyes blazed with madness.

'You're lying!'

'It's a glass replica, you poor fool,' I said. 'Do you imagine I

186

would let you and your moronic brother walk off with a million dollars worth of diamonds?'

She drew in her breath in a sharp, little hiss.

I expected her to fly into a murderous rage but what I had told her seemed to crush her.

'I warned the mug,' she said, half to herself. 'I knew you were a snake from the moment I saw you, but he wouldn't listen. "This guy's okay," he kept saying, but I knew different.' She relaxed back. 'Okay, Mr. Cheapie Carr, so you win. If they catch me, I'll go away for life. I've already had eight years in jail. I know what it means . . . you don't. Fel didn't He's lucky to be dead.'

I couldn't bear to look at her any longer.

'Beat it!' I said. 'When they pick you up, talk as much as you like. I've got beyond caring. Get out and get lost!'

She didn't seem to hear me.

'I had two weeks shut up in his stinking pad,' she said. 'Two weeks! Every minute I expected the fuzz to come and get me. God! I could do with a drink!' She pressed her hands to her face. Watching her, I felt no pity for her. I wanted to be rid of her, to drive away, to go back to Paradise City and wait there for the police to come and get me.

'Beat it!' I shouted at her. 'You're rotten. Even a stinking brainless creep like Spooky doesn't want you! Get the hell away from me!'

'Fel was the only one who couldn't live without me,' she said. 'Then he ran away when the crunch came . . . yellow right through.' She gave a hard barking laugh. 'Well, I guess this is curtains for me . . . I wonder what it's like to be dead.'

Then I saw she had my gun in her hand.

'Drop that!' I shouted.

'So long, Cheapie . . . your time will come.' As I lunged at her, she shoved me off, lifted the gun, pointed it at her head and pulled the trigger.

The flash of the gun blinded me and the bang stunned me. I felt a wet mess on my face and shuddering I threw myself out of the car. I stood there shaking, mopping my face with my handkerchief as a thin wisp of gun smoke curled out of the open door.

Sergeant O'Halloran sat at his desk, rolling his pencil across the blotter.

On the bench against the wall sat five of Spooky's gang: kids ranging from ten to fifteen years of age, sullen, dirty and wearing their uniform of black shirts and jeans.

I caused a sensation with these kids as the two patrolmen shoved me into the charge-room: that I could understand. With my candy floss wig at the back of my head, Rhea's blood on my shirt, a bruise on the side of my jaw where one of the patrolmen had hit me and handcuffs on my wrists I made a photo that would cause a sensation anywhere.

There was an immediate buzz from the kids and O'Halloran, leaning forward, bawled, 'Quiet, you little bastards! Hear me or I'll get amongst you!'

It seemed to me I was back on square A.

One of the patrolmen came forward and began talking to O'Halloran. I only caught a few of his words: 'Tamiami Trail ... shot dead ... gun in his hand ...' Lowering his voice, he went on talking and O'Halloran wrote it all down.

I knew he was booking me for Rhea's murder and I didn't care. I was past caring about anything. During the long drive back to Luceville I had had time to think. Rhea's suicide had jolted me back to the man I had been before the crash that had killed Judy. Now, I saw myself as I was. This subconscious greed that must have always been with me had come to the surface. Because of this greed I had caused Sydney's death. Because of this greed I had murdered Fel Morgan. I thought of the moment when I had hooked my fingers into his trousers' cuffs and had heaved him into oblivion.

This moment, as I was driven back to Luceville, was my moment of truth.

Finally, O'Halloran got through with his writing, then he beckoned to me. I didn't move. I stared at him until the patrolman guarding me, gave me a shove forward.

'Your name?' O'Halloran demanded in his worn-out husky

voice.

'Laurence fifteen-hundred-dollars Carr,' I told him.

He leaned forward, his little pig eyes opening wide, then he seemed to recognise me.

'Take that goddamn wig off,' he said to the patrolman who pulled the wig off my head and put it on the desk.

O'Halloran drew in a long, slow breath, then staring at me, he said. 'You got anything to say, but watch it, whatever you say could be used against you.'

'She was as sick of life as I am,' I said. 'She wanted to die so I shot her.'

He snorted, then sat back, waving to the patrolman. 'He's a nutter. Take him to Homicide.'

So I was taken to the Homicide department. The Lieutenant in charge was a small, white-haired man with steel blue eyes, a red face and an aggressive jaw.

He asked a lot of questions, but by this time I wasn't in the mood to talk. I sat dumb, staring down at the floor and even when he slapped me across the face, I still said nothing. So, finally, they put me in a cell.

I sat there, hating myself because I had caused the death of a man who had gone so much for me and who had left me the bulk of his riches.

They brought me a meal which I didn't eat.

Later, O'Halloran came into the cell and with his thumbs hooked into his belt, he regarded me.

'You're in real trouble buster,' he said and his husky voice sounded surprisingly gentle. 'What did you want to sound off for? There's still time ... suppose you give it to me the way it happened?'

I looked directly at him.

'I killed her,' I said. 'The rest of the performance is up to you people.'

O'Halloran scratched under his right armpit.

'The Lieutenant wants to know if you'll make a statement.' He shifted his cap to the back of his head. 'Listen, buster, if I were you, I wouldn't, but I'm doing what I'm told.'

I could see he was worried.

189

'Why wouldn't you?' I asked.

He took off his cap, stared at it, then slapped it on his head.

'Between you and me, I think you're a nutter and I don't believe you knocked her off. That's why I think you should sit tight and keep your trap shut until you get an attorney here.'

'You think I'm a nutter?'

He nodded.

'Yeah ... all along. The moment you hit this town, that's what I thought. Now take my advice. You sit tight. We've called Paradise City. There's a bit shot attorney coming with your partner, Mr. Luce. They'll fix this. You sit tight.'

The last thing I wanted was for Tom Luce to get me out of this mess.

'Tell the Lieutenant I'm now ready to make a statement.'

O'Halloran shifted from one foot to the other.

'Look, fella, you may be a nutter, but you have something I dig for.' He leaned forward and lowering his voice, he went on. 'You don't understand the trouble you're in. Look ... suppose I call Miss Baxter and tell her ... she'll help you. How's that, fella?'

Jenny?

I saw now that Jenny had gone the way Judy had gone ... a wonderful memory, a dream, but no longer for me.

'Tell the Lieutenant I'll make a statement,' I said.

O'Halloran wiped the sweat off his face with the back of his hand.

'You could talk yourself into a fifteen year stretch,' he said and I could see he was really worried. 'Even if they think you're a nutter, you couldn't get out under ten.'

I leaned back against the prison wall, suddenly relaxed.

'Tell the Lieutenant I'll make a statement.' In my mind I saw Sydney with his kindness and his talents, buzzing around me. 'Fifteen years ... ten years? Well, it will make a change of scene, won't it?'

AN ACE UP MY SLEEVE
by James Hadley Chase

An Ace Up My Sleeve is a story of blackmail. It is a story of three people, all out for one thing: all determined to do anything to get it.

It is a story of bluff and counter-bluff – a game which develops into a deadly battle of violence and extortion.

From the moment Helga Rolfe, the elegant wife of one of the richest of tycoons, picks up a gum-chewing boy, young enough to be her son, events jump, bank and skid through a series of 180 degree turns and hair-raising gambits, racing to a climax of shattering impact – for both winners and losers . . .

0 552 09424 2   £1.75

MALLORY
by James Hadley Chase

A small French resistance group came to London after the war to avenge the death of their leader, betrayed to the Gestapo by one of their own members. But the traitor, Mallory, proved more than a match for them, and two corpses later, the remaining three called in outside help. They chose Martin Corridon, an ex-commando, who accepted the job planned a neat double-cross of his own once he had the money. But it didn't quite work out that way: Corridon found himself trailing Mallory from the dens of Soho to the wilds of a remote Scottish island . . .

0 552 10765 4   £1.75

CRIMES TITLE AVAILABLE FROM CORGI BOOKS

While every effort is made to keep prices low, it is sometimes necessary to increase prices at short notice. Corgi Books reserve the right to show new retail prices on covers which may differ from those previously advertised in the text or elsewhere.

The prices shown below were correct at the time of going to press.

☐	10426 4	JOKER IN THE PACK	*James Hadley Chase* £1.50
☐	11558 4	WELL NOW MY PRETTY	*James Hadley Chase* £1.50
☐	11356 5	THE WAY THE COOKIE CRUMBLES	*James Hadley Chase* £1.50
☐	10522 8	NO ORCHID'S FOR MISS BLANDISH	*James Hadley Chase* £1.50
☐	10574 0	DO ME A FAVOUR, DROP DEAD	*James Hadley Chase* £1.50
☐	11646 7	COME EASY, GO EASY	*James Hadley Chase* 95p
☐	11506 1	BELIEVED VIOLENT	*James Hadley Chase* £1.50
☐	09648 2	HAVE A CHANGE OF SCENE	*James Hadley Chase* £1.75
☐	10765 4	MALLORY	*James Hadley Chase* £1.75
☐	09424 2	AN ACE UP MY SLEEVE	*James Hadley Chase* £1.75
☐	10328 4	LADY, HERE'S YOUR WREATH	*James Hadley Chase* £1.75
☐	12021 9	RUMPELSTILTSKIN	*Ed McBain* £1.50
☐	12203 3	BEAUTY AND THE BEAST	*Ed McBain* £1.75

ORDER FORM

All these books are available at your book shop or newsagent, or can be ordered direct from the publisher. Just tick the titles you want and fill in the form below.

CORGI BOOKS, Cash Sales Department, P.O. Box 11, Falmouth, Cornwall.

Please send cheque or postal order, no currency.

Please allow cost of book(s) plus the following for postage and packing:

U.K. Customers—Allow 55p for the first book, 22p for the second book and 14p for each additional book ordered, to a maximum charge of £1.75.

B.F.P.O. and Eire—Allow 55p for the first book, 22p for the second book plus 14p per copy for the next seven books, thereafter 8p per book.

Overseas Customers—Allow £1.00 for the first book and 25p per copy for each additional book.

NAME (Block Letters) ....

ADDRESS ....

....